JEMEZ BRAND

For hundreds of years, the Jemez high country of New Mexico has been steeped in rumor and legend. Some say one of the original Seven Golden Cities of the Cibola Indians was once there, sought by Spanish conquistadors. In more recent times, stories of men having gone missing along the fabled Rio Del Gato — the River of the Cat — have become part of local folklore. When Preacher Devlin discovers two murdered men with the face of a cat cut into their palms, and then surreptitiously observes a small band of Indians traveling through a canyon — led by a woman wearing a gold cat's-head mask — he reckons he's stumbled upon something extraordinary. With an ethnologist as his new companion, Devlin must fend off gunslinging fortune-hunters in a race to be the first to unravel the secret of the lost Cibola gold.

JEMEZ BRAND

L. L. FOREMAN

SAGEBRUSH
Large Print Westerns

First published in the United States by Ace Books

First Isis Edition
published 2019
by arrangement with
Golden West Literary Agency

A catalogue record for this book is available
from the British Library.

ISBN 978-1-78541-686-6 (pb)

Published by
F. A. Thorpe (Publishing)
Anstey, Leicestershire

Set by Words & Graphics Ltd.
Anstey, Leicestershire
Printed and bound in Great Britain by
T. J. International Ltd., Padstow, Cornwall

This book is printed on acid-free paper

PART ONE

CHAPTER
ONE

The rifle was a good one — a Ballard Military .54 — and it had been fired empty. A fine Visalia saddle hung racked on a low black oak branch, its stirrup straps neatly folded back over the seat and the matched silver-mounted bridle hooked over the big Spanish-style horn. A thick Navaho saddle blanket had been laid first over the branch, to keep the rough bark from skinning the saddle pads. Two woolen blankets and a new tarp made up the bed, and a large canteen stood at the foot of the oak in the shade.

This was the camp of a well-provided and careful man. It had been pitched in a thicket, in a small space surrounded by the black oaks and thick brush overlooking the deep canyon of the Rio Del Gato. The camper lay across the blankets and tarp, under the light of the full moon, and he did not stir when the big man in somber black bent over him. He couldn't move, and he never would again of his own volition. He was dead. His horse, a good-looking grulla gelding, also lay dead.

The dead man lay with his face to the moon, his arms spread out, and his hands turned upward as if in a gesture of mute supplication. The palm of his left hand had been cut six times, and the six little cuts were arranged in the form of a strange pattern — a crude caricature of a face with pointed ears. A thin blue bruise marked a line around the dead man's neck, the kind of bruise that a tight noose could have left.

This was murder. As such, it did not greatly concern the big man in black, for he was not squeamish, not devoted to law and order, and had never before set eyes on the victim. But some of its aspects were bizarre enough to intrigue his curiosity. He concluded tentatively that there was the possibility of a crazy man on the loose somewhere hereabouts in the high Jemez country of New Mexico. It was hardly reasonable to suppose that any sane man would go to the trouble of laying out his victim across the blankets, cut that weird arrangement of an eared face on the palm of the left hand, and then go off without taking the perfectly good rifle and expensive saddle. But when he studied the scene more closely, and detected the tracks of more than one pair of feet in the dirt, the black-garbed man frowned and revised his first conclusion.

They were shallow tracks lacking sharp outline and obviously had been made during or soon after a recent rain. At this altitude it could almost be counted upon to rain for an hour or two every afternoon during most of the early summer. This meant that the victim had not long been dead. Nor did he yet have the sunken look that a day-old corpse would be expected to have. He had a short but compactly built body, and a knotty kind of face that had not been shaved very lately. From his general appearance he could have been either a lawman or a capable gunman, but not a working cowman or sheepman. His clothes were good, and around his middle were belted a pair of hand-tooled holsters, both empty. His assassins had taken his six-guns, but left untouched his rifle and saddle, and apparently had not even disturbed his pockets.

"A none too profitable kind o' killin', this," murmured the big man, and that, to his strictly material way of thinking, meant that it was none too sensible.

He felt in the dead man's pockets, found some loose change and a roll of bills, and sat on his heels to think it over. It was not his habit to inquire into all the illegalities and dark doings that cropped up in his path, for his own career was generously spotted with them, but this was a challenge for any man's brain power.

He was a tall man, broad across the shoulders and long in the arms and legs, and his knee-length coat and wide-brimmed hat were as black as his waiting horse. The coat, cut along austere lines, was of good broadcloth and fairly well worn. The hat had a flat brim and crown. Both carried a strong suggestion of the pulpit. A black string tie and plain riding boots added to the illusion of clerical pursuits, but when he sat on his heels, two gun butts poked bulges in the tails of his long coat, and he had large and muscular hands fashioned for the efficient manipulation of whatever they might happen to grasp. And his face, being what it was, would have proved no asset to a clergyman. It lacked benignity and trustfulness. Strength and a saturnine twist of humor were its dominant features, laid upon a foundation of cool toughness. His hard mouth was wide and flat-lipped, and his well-defined

5

nose bannered the quality of easy arrogance. Altogether a piratical, hawkish face, lean and dark, with deep-set slaty eyes wherein latent violence lurked like a scalding force in a deceptively quiet geyser.

His trade-marks were on him for wise and knowledgeable eyes to read: A lobo long rider, and a master of the various specialized crafts that kept him alive and ahead of the multiple dangers that everlastingly haunted his wayward trail.

Chewing slowly on the end of an unlighted Mexican cigar of dubious hue, he took note of the empty brass shells scattered near the foot of the black oak. "Put up a fight, but they were too good for him, whoever they were," he mused, and then his slaty eyes stilled and went chilly after his ears told him of something he needed to know. Without rising from his heels, he lunged in a low dive for the black oak trunk.

His dive was a streak of movement without any waste motion, and the gunshot that flashed from a tangle of locust shrub was lined a mite too high to get him. The bullet sang a long and screeching note across the river canyon, and as the big man whirled behind the tree trunk he had one heavy-barreled gun out in his hand with the hammer thumbed back. His black horse, standing with reins grounded and ears cocked, threw up its head and snorted, disliking the shattering of the night's peace and quiet. The long-barreled six-gun lined fast on the locust patch and roared twice, and somebody there bit off a short, pained cry.

The big man clicked the hammer back for another shot, and took aim at the place where he had sent the others. He spoke an uncompromising command, his voice harsh. "Show y'self right quick, hombre — or take bad medicine!"

Nobody showed, but somebody mumbled in a tired and dragging voice: "I already took it plenty, mister! You sure deal it out promiscuous. Got me both times — both arms."

"That don't stop you walkin'. Come out o' there!"

"A'right, I'm comin'. Hold your smoke off an' gimme time. It ain't no cinch to get up with your arms busted."

After a floundering and a breaking of brush, a lanky man came slouching out, both arms bloody and dangling, his dirt-smeared face grayish. He kept a pair of sick and bloodshot eyes fastened on the tall man, and he wagged his head disgustedly.

"Hell's clinkers!" he said, in the bitterly resigned way of a man showing two pairs to four aces. "Ain't it just my cussed luck to shoot at a dog an' stir up a bear! Here I prowl for hours through the damnedest kind o' thorny brush to get a crack at Soldier Smith — an' I run slam bang into no less'n Preacher Devlin! Howdy, Preacher. We met once in Nogales, in the Blue Steer one night. You busted a combine o' slick tinhorns, a monte layout, an' all the lights. I was a bouncer there, an' you bounced me over the bar. 'Member?"

Devlin didn't recall the incident, it being merely a minor note in a long and stormy symphony, but it sounded reasonable. The lanky man noticed the body on the blankets, then, and he sucked in his lips.

7

"Is Soldier dead? You got him, too?" The swift query contained a tense eagerness. It was as if he badly wanted to be assured of the manner in which the man had died, rather than the matter of the death itself. "He's the one I was sent to cut down." A shadow of fear crossed his grayed face. "I didn't hear no shot, comin' up."

Preacher Devlin, sky-limit gambler, master gun fighter, and man of more special notoriety and known misdeeds than he could have wished for had he been running for election as hell's representative, eyed the wounded man. He reflected that maybe candor was still a virtue, even when it embraced admission of contemplated murder. "No," he answered. "No, I didn't gun this here Soldier Smith or whatever you called him. Seems he didn't die that way. Who're you?"

"Epp Redrick," said the lanky man mechanically, and stared at the body. He showed visible signs of losing what nerve he had left. "Soldier wasn't shot, you say? You sure?"

"Take a look at his neck. He's got a rope mark all round it. Hanged, reckon. If he was any kin to you, hombre, I'd say he was the right candidate for it!"

Redrick swallowed, the muscles of his skinny throat working up and down. He began edging away. "He wasn't hanged," he muttered, still staring at the dead Soldier Smith. "They got him!"

"Who got him?"

"*They* did. You know, Preacher, so why ask me? You're up here after the same game we are, ain't you? What else would you be here for?"

Devlin didn't trouble to answer that question. It would have entailed some explanation dealing with the matter of a crooked cattle buyer who had reached out too far and got himself damaged, an ensuing fast ride, and a consequently annoyed sheriffs posse. The Preacher was not in a mood to engage in idle reminiscences.

"You're shakin' like a kicked colt," he said. "What're you scared of, besides me?"

"Who wouldn't be scared o' what he got?" gulped Redrick, nodding down at the silent body on the blankets. "You stick around here if you want, Preacher, but me, I'm gettin' out o' this cussed spot fast as hell lets me!"

"You'll bleed to death," Devlin pointed out, not too concernedly. "Better let me tie up those holes I shot in you. What did this Soldier Smith do, that you wanted to gun him so bad? An' who are the others you spoke of?"

"Nev' mind that. I was a damn fool to come brush-dustin' up here alone. They won't never get me doin' that again! You gonna let me go, Preacher? If we hang around here we'll both sure — Glory blazes, look! His hand! They put the cat face on him!"

Devlin nodded. "Yeah, I saw that. Cat, you say? Hm-m-m. Now you mention it, it does look like a cat's face."

"Sure!" Redrick's face was grayer than ever. "You don't know about it? A'right . . . a'right. You stay here. You'll learn! Shoot if you want, but here I go!" He turned and stumbled hurriedly off, threading his way through the brushy thickets and veering up the slope of the high ridge away from the deep river canyon.

It was Devlin's decided opinion that there was just too much mystery around here, and no particular prospect of profit to warrant any of it. To speculate upon an unusual killing was fair exercise for the mental faculties, but to delve seriously into it was unprofitable, and one's strictest attention, he considered, should not wander too far from one's pocket. The world was full of brainy men who let their academic interests sidetrack them into poverty. He took a last look at the dead man, shrugged, and turned to his horse.

Mounting, he remembered the murdered man's roll of bills, gave it some study, and finally decided to leave it. It was not that he entertained any superstitions about a dead man's cash, and scruples were no botheration to him, but he did have a certain code of self-respect which demanded that he earn what he got, one way or another and insofar as possible. There was a fine distinction, as he saw it, between taking from a live man and pilfering from a helpless dead one. He picked up his reins and prepared to push on over toward Arizona way, south along the border country where the folks were a little less fussy about the casual shooting of a crooked cattle buyer.

CHAPTER
TWO

Something made a strange sound behind the Preacher, a faint whirring sound. Certain it was a fast-thrown knife, he ducked off his horse. He was in a cold anger when he hit the ground with his feet, and he heard the whirring sound whisper overhead. It changed its note and ended, but there was another whir sounding off just like it farther away. Then that one ended, more abruptly and without changing its note, and when he looked around for Redrick he saw the man toppling into a narrow arroyo that gashed the slope, limp as a sawdust doll. It was only a glimpse, and Redrick suddenly and amazingly appeared to have grown a pair of extra ears.

Devlin headed on the run for the arroyo. He chose his ground as he went, keeping his head low and eyes alert, but before he made half the distance a burst of shots crashed furiously from the rim of the canyon off to his left. Echoes from the canyon doubled the uproar, and what once had been a reasonably quiet night now boomed and flamed like a battlefield. Only the moon remained unchanged, big and pale and serene in the sky, casting a light that made every shadow look like a black patch on silver.

The Preacher swore surprisedly, flipped his guns from under his ministerial coat, and looked for something to shoot at. Three bullets came close enough to convince him that the unknown bushwhackers had the range and were out to do business. He dropped flat behind a brush-fringed hummock and listened to twigs being shot off above his head. With controlled patience he waited for the first salvo to slacken, drew himself up a trifle and with his own long-barreled guns blazed a return salute. He caught sight of a black head, saw it jerk back when he fired, and he repeated on the next.

"Two down," he checked, and dropped another with a fast chop shot. They weren't possemen or bounty hunters, he was sure of that. Dusky faces and long black hair just didn't generally belong in a sheriffs posse.

For good measure, and to give the long-haired enthusiasts an idea of what could be done with honest guns, Devlin methodically shot at white tufa stones atop the canyon rim and exploded the brittle chunks into chalky fragments. Reloading, he bided his time to let that example of accurate shooting sink in, and was greeted by a long silence. He ran his eye along the ragged and moonlight-tipped scar of the arroyo which coursed its way into the canyon, and speculated about it. It was highly possible, he figured, that the enemy might be snaking up along that arroyo to get around him from farther up the slope. A bank of clouds was ponderously sailing up to meet the full moon, and maybe the long-haired ones were watching that, waiting for the moonlight to be shut off for a while.

12

"A devil of a mess to get into, this!" he muttered, and trimmed his frayed cigar with his strong white teeth. "Seems like all the folks around here spend their time gunnin' for each other — whites an' Injuns, an' maybe a few in-betweens. What the blazes started all this anyway?"

When deep murkiness came with the hiding of the moon, the Preacher eased from his cover and continued warily on to the arroyo. The silence had gone unbroken. Now he could hear nothing, not even the river below, which flowed in a broad and smooth ribbon along through here for several miles before it entered the wider valley of the Calaveras to the southeast. Gaining the arroyo, Devlin dropped into it, and found Redrick lying at the bottom on the wet gravel bed.

Epp Redrick was stone-dead, as dead as Soldier Smith, and from the same weird and deadly cause. Devlin crouched motionless and listened for long moments before he took a chance on striking a match. Under the tiny flare he studied the bluish bruise that circled Redrick's scrawny neck. This one hadn't met his finish by hanging, that was certain, despite the evidence of the rope bruise. Nor had he been knifed or shot dead. Devlin turned over the limp, grimed hands. There on the left palm, gashed sketchily with the point of a knife, was that cat's face again.

"Damnedest brand I ever saw on man or cow," Devlin mused, and continued his noiseless way on down the arroyo.

Descending with wary circumspection, he followed the arroyo down into the canyon, desirous of taking a look at the long-haired men whom he had shot and to find out something about them. They hadn't been Navahos, he felt, nor Pueblo Indians. The Navahos had been behaving themselves for a good many years, and it took desperate reasons to push them into violent trouble.

The nearest Pueblo Indians were the Cochuritis, just north of the Calaveras Valley. They, like all the farming Pueblos, tended their corn crops and sheep, and minded their own business. That left only the Apaches, or the possibility of a straying band of some other Plains tribe. But Plains Indians avoided night fighting, believing that a man killed at night spent all eternity thereafter in darkness. Besides, no Plains warrior could have resisted the impulse to let out at least one healthy war whoop as he blazed away.

A prowling search of the canyon floor revealed nothing except the certainty that the dead or wounded had been borne off by their comrades. The illogical aspects of the whole affair irritated the Preacher, but the lack of visible motive failed to convince him that none existed. The more hidden the motive, the deeper it went, and he was now beginning to suspect the existence of something pretty big around here.

With all the sharp experience and observations of a tempestuous life to back him, it was his judgment that few men plunged earnestly into violence without a strong reason, and the strongest reasons usually embraced some form of personal profit. Those long-haired shooters had been very much in earnest. So had Redrick, for that matter, and probably Soldier

Smith, too. They had taken chances and dealt lightly with life, for good reasons known to themselves.

Profit — that was the motive and the spur. Redrick had let slip something of the kind, before he tried to flee from the little hidden camp in the thicket. He had mentioned other men and a game in which they were all involved. Somebody possessed something well worth the risk of taking, and other unknowns were out to get it. The blue death mark, the cat's face and other imponderables were merely adjuncts to the main riddle.

Being what he was — a gambler in every phase of life, willing at any time to buy chips in any sky-limit game that came his way — Preacher Devlin hankered to get a look at the jackpot and the size of the prospective profit.

It was too dark to search for tracks, but the moon was coming out from behind the cloud bank, and that would give light enough when it appeared. The high canyon walls were mostly red rock palisades, rising almost sheer on both sides, and there was very little floor left at the bottom by the river. The Preacher ran his eyes up the cliff.

"Steep as a horse's face," he pronounced it, and gave some due credit to those who had clambered up it to shoot at him over the rim. The river was a shining black band, its flow so smooth that the water looked stationary, barely rippling here and there where it passed over unseen rocks in the bed.

In the early spring, when the mountain snows melted and the heavy rains came, this twenty-mile length of deep canyon was probably a raging gorge, and even in

15

the driest summers it likely never fell much below its present depth. Rain was the master and maker of topography in this kind of country, and rang the changes with a restless hand, but a solid red rock canyon like this one of the Rio Del Gato could defy it and remain unaltered for a thousand years.

Prospects of finding tracks on the scant bit of gravelly beach did not look promising. The moon showed itself again, but failed to help. Devlin stood and chewed on his cigar.

"Wish I'd made that Redrick hombre spill all he knew about —" A muffled wisp of sound along the river broke into his wish, and he stepped softly back into the deep shadow of the canyon wall. Some kind of boat was coming down river. Soon the Preacher sighted the outline of it against the dark shine of the water, a narrow thing that had the shape of a canoe. As it drew nearer he made it out to be considerably longer than had appeared at first glimpse. Several figures moved in unison in it, paddling with scarcely a splash. To find a canoe up here in the New Mexico mountains was an unusual occurrence.

One figure stood forward in the pointed bow, a slender figure not as dark as the rest. It had a pale-yellow face and head that caught some of the moon's reflection and gave off a polished and gleaming luminousness. The canoe came gliding on, the silent paddlers now stilled to let it drift to the small strip of beach, and the yellow face merged into clearer moonlight.

16

The Preacher stopped chewing, and stared. For once in his life he considered the possibility that maybe a man's past misdeeds could catch up with him and commit low-down tricks upon his eyes and brain. But this was no hallucination, and Devlin's consideration of retribution was brief. The yellow face was golden — not merely the color, but the metal. It had narrow, slanted eyes, a blunt nose, and pointed ears. It was the face of a cat, a golden cat, on the slender and dainty body of a very scantily clad woman.

"What in thunder!" murmured the Preacher, and he wondered if this was the jackpot. That golden head was valuable, if solid.

The long canoe floated to the shore and was carefully grounded. Its dark occupants silently disembarked. They were naked except for loincloths and moccasins, but leather bandoleers were slung across their shoulders, and each man carried a rifle. Devlin counted eleven of them, and he decided that eleven rifles were somewhat too many to stir up, what with the lack of cover for himself and limited space to operate in. He kept to the shadows, his eyes half closed to shield their cold shine, and his hands on his gun butts.

The dark men lifted the canoe farther up onto the beach and set it down, all without a word spoken. Then straightening up, they turned their faces toward a taller figure in ragged trousers who gestured curtly in the direction of the arroyo, where it entered the canyon. Led by the trousered man and the cat-headed woman, they softly padded up the arroyo in single file, and the last of them vanished. Devlin gave them plenty of time to make progress up the arroyo before he stepped out of the shadows and moved to the canoe.

He barely had time to begin looking the canoe over before a steady splashing told him of somebody wading the skirt of the river. The canoe had come from upstream, but this noise approached from the other direction. It struck the Preacher that this canyon of the Rio Del Gato was considerable of a busy thoroughfare at night. Withdrawing to the shadows again, he stood watch.

A humped figure loomed up, wading the shallow edge with no attempt at caution, and stepped onto the beach. This one was a fully clothed white man, and the hump was caused by the pack that he carried strapped to his back. The newcomer seated himself with an audible sigh of relief, and began tugging off his soaked boots. Happening to turn his face toward the beached canoe, and for the first time seeing what it was, he went motionless.

"Well, now, I'll be damned!" he exclaimed in mild surprise, and he had the voice of a young man.

The Preacher spoke in a murmur from the shadows. "You'll be damned dead, young feller, if you don't keep quiet!"

The man sprang up nimbly, for all the weight of his hefty pack, one boot still on, the other in his hand. "Huh? Did I hear somebody speak?"

"It wasn't any echo," said Devlin. "Yank that boot back on an' come over here! This way. Quiet, now. That's fine. Keep your hands where I can see 'em. You on the gun for Soldier Smith, too?"

18

"What?" The young man stared uncomprehendingly. "Of course not. Who are you? My name's Roud Connell. I'm an ethnologist. I'm searching for Indian rock pictures and relics — things like that, you know."

Devlin quirked a black and quizzical eyebrow. "Some queer fish in this river tonight!" was his comment. "Canoe Injuns from nowhere, a cat-faced female, an' now — What did you call yourself?"

"An ethnologist. The scientific study of the various human races and their origins, and all that, you know," Roud Connell explained, with the patient manner of a man who had often had to explain his profession to the unenlightened. "I specialize in the native Amerinds, Indians of the American continent. Have you happened to notice any signs of Indian culture in this region?"

"I've seen Injuns," drawled Devlin, "but I wouldn't say they were exactly cultured."

He studied the young scientist. The fellow was obviously honest, judging by his frank face and eyes, and probably he was what he claimed to be. A well-set-up young specimen, he seemed, and no pale scholar. He was tanned and healthy, and the easy way he bore that heavy pack bespoke hard muscles and a good pair of legs. He wore no weapon of any kind in sight.

"Are those rock pictures so wild an' shy that you got to sneak up on 'em in the dark?" Devlin queried reasonably.

Roud Connell grinned, and when he did that he looked more human than ever. "Well, not quite. I left my camp early this morning, and I was too far up this canyon to turn back when it got dark. I've got a horse and a pack mule down in Calaveras Valley, but I came on foot up here because I can climb around better that way. When the dark caught me, I pushed on, looking for some spot where I could climb out and camp for the night. I wasn't tired then. It's a devil of a canyon to get out of. Practically no beach anywhere for miles. This spot looks all right, though."

"I don't recommend it," said Devlin. "Too public, an' the folks around here don't seem friendly to strangers for some reason."

Roud Connell nodded politely, but began removing his pack, nevertheless. "I've had dealings with a good many distrustful Indians. A few gifts of tobacco usually loosen them up."

"These Injuns don't make that kind o' smoke," Devlin remarked dryly. "There's a couple of hombres back over the rim who could tell you that, if they weren't dead!"

"Dead? Killed, do you mean? Say, you also made some mention of a cat-headed female a little while ago." Roud Connell sent the tall gun fighter a searching and peculiar look. "Uh . . . are you up here for your health, or on business?"

"Both," said Devlin tersely. "But the business cropped up after I got here. Listen. I hear the local folks comin' back down. She'll be with 'em."

"You mean the cat-headed female? Impossible! Why, my dear Mr . . . uh . . . what did you say your name is?"

"Devlin," said the Preacher, listening to the faint padding of moccasins coming down the arroyo.

Roud Connell sent the notorious long rider a different kind of look, a long and close look that took in the details of the austere black garb and flinty face. "Oh!" he said. I've . . . er . . . heard of you, I think, here and there. Saw a poster recently, too, tacked up outside a —"

"Don't try to cash in on it!" murmured the Preacher pleasantly. "I wouldn't want to rob science of a worker. Ps-sst. Quiet! Here they come. Get back here an' freeze!"

CHAPTER
THREE

First to appear from the mouth of the arroyo was the man in ragged trousers, treading softly on the balls of his moccasined feet and carrying a pistol in his hand. Then, close behind him, the slender, shapely figure of the woman, surmounted by the luminously shining head of polished gold, the calm expression of the feline face unchanged. And finally the little procession of silent walkers, bearing two long burdens among them.

The party trooped down to the boat, carried it to the river's edge, and placed the two burdens in it. They boarded the boat carefully, and pushed off. As silently as they had come, they paddled back upstream against the current, and Devlin heard Roud Connell release a long, pent-up breath of stunned amazement.

"It's . . . it's incredible!" Connell gasped shakily. "That woman . . . or girl . . . whatever she is — I've simply got to investigate her!"

"You'll get your scientific head clawed off yet, you go prancing up to that cat lady!" Devlin informed him. "Hold your voice down. Let's tail after 'em an' see can we find where they hole up. C'mon, Rowdy!"

Together they slipped along the foot of the high canyon cliff, trying to keep the canoe in sight, but the

22

strip of beach land ran out and water came up over their boot tops. The canoe glided rapidly on around a bend and out of sight. Roud Connell was all for wading on until his hat floated, but the Preacher got a hold on his shirt and yanked him back.

"Too much splash," Devlin growled. "Anyway, I don't feel like swimmin' that current, gold cats or no gold cats."

Roud Connell retreated to the bank, sat on a rock, and stared dazedly before him. "Fantastic!" he muttered, evidently attempting to match the facts against his ethnological knowledge. "Why, I never would have believed that wild bunch of rumors, but this — Jumping Jupiter! Can it actually be true? The Rio Del Gato — River of the Cat! The lost Tewa tribe — the lost Tewa treasures, and the Tewa Cat! And all those crazy rumors about the men who —"

"Treasures, did you say?" Devlin interrupted. He had come upon many such legends. New Mexico and the Southwest abounded with them at all times, each tale a juicy bait for gullible greenhorns to swallow. But that golden head was visible evidence of something or other in this particular case, and the Preacher believed in keeping an open and receptive mind in such matters.

Tugging off his water-logged boots, Roud looked at the gun fighter. "Have you ever come across the rumor that several men have gone missing along this river from time to time?" he asked. "I have, and I traced it to the Cochuriti village. But those Cochuritis won't talk about this canyon. Just the mention of it freezes them up. I put it down to old superstition, but I'm not so sure now that they haven't got good reason to be afraid of this place."

"Aren't you mixin' a little law work with your purely scientific interests?" Devlin hinted.

Roud shook his head. "No. I've investigated this old river pretty thoroughly from historical records and other sources, and I found tales concerning it that were so lurid I laughed at them. Science must be skeptical, you know, and I'm interested only in proven facts. But I'm convinced that it was somewhere along here that the last of the Tewa Indians became extinct. Naturally, I'm interested in anything that has to do with this region, and that's how I stumbled upon these rumors about missing men. And that's why I'm here."

"What kind of Injuns did you say? Never heard of 'em."

"I'm not surprised," said Roud. "Most of them, I think, were killed by the Spaniards three hundred years ago. The survivors took refuge in the mountains, and that was the last ever heard of them. The Tewa pueblo, or village, may actually have been one of the original Seven Golden Cities of the Cibola that so many Spanish adventurers sought in vain up here north of the Rio Grande. Of course, I'm verging into the semilegendary in guessing at that. But who's to judge definitely just where legend ends and truth begins?"

"Nobody that I know." Devlin stated solemnly. "The world's too full o' liars. What about that treasure cache you spoke of?"

But Roud Connell was not to be diverted from his ethnological theme by any query dealing with mere

24

treasure. "Indian culture, you see," he explained, "had its central point in Peru, as far as we know. From there, through various migrations, it spread northward. Naturally, the farther it spread from the central cultural point, the more primitive and weakened the culture, until we find savage barbarians and wild nomads on the fringe, such as the Apaches and some other warlike tribes. You understand?"

"Perfectly. What about that treasure?"

"Now, we know that a few spots or 'islands' of Indian culture continued to flourish," Roud went on, ignoring the question. "When the first Spaniards entered this region they found quite a high degree of civilization among the Pueblo tribes. The Spaniards won the country, but some of the Pueblo people fled before them into the mountains. It's known from old Spanish records that a party of armed Spaniards pursued an Indian band, believing that the Indians were carrying gold with them that they had mined for centuries. These Indians may have been Tewas. I have reason to believe they were. They escaped, but they were discovered the following year on a river which the Spaniards later named Rio Del Gato — River of the Cat. There was a battle. Most of the Indians fell, some were captured, and a few got away. The Spaniards found no gold."

"Have you got any idea what came of it?" Devlin prodded.

Roud gave him a grin. "Interested, aren't you? So am I, but my interest is in tracing the history of the Tewas, rather than their gold. Those Tewas, you see, were remarkable in some ways. Like the ancient Egyptians, they seem to have had a religious reverence for the cat — probably the wild cat in the case of the Tewas, or possibly a conventionalized picture form that had come down to them through the ages. We don't know where the Indian race originally sprang from, after all. They may have come from Egypt, thousands of years ago, or perhaps they traveled here to this continent by way of the so-called Lost Atlantis. Who knows?"

"I don't, for one," admitted the Preacher. "So the Spaniards never found any cache, huh?"

"Never," Roud answered, "although they did manage to worm a clue out of the Indians they captured. Apparently only the Indian tribal heads were intrusted with hiding the treasures. They did a good job of it. All they told the rest was, 'It is in the eye of the golden cat that slumbers by the river,' and this was all that the captives could tell the Spaniards. My father, by the way, came up here to investigate several years ago. He was an ethnologist, too. I'm taking up where he left off."

"Did he find anything?"

"I don't know. He never came back. I always believed that he must have had an accident and drowned, but now — Well, I don't know. According to rumor, other men have vanished on this river within the last few years. And now those two you mentioned. You saw them?"

Devlin nodded. "So did you. Those canoe Injuns were carryin' both bodies when they pulled out. Both men were on the prowl up here, lookin' for what they could find. One, name o' Redrick, seemed to savvy

26

somethin' o' what you've been lecturin' me about, so maybe it's not such a close secret. I've got a notion there are others on the hunt for that Tewa gold — an' they're ready to shoot for it. Soldier Smith, the other dead un, struck me as a tough little hombre on the lone prowl. Redrick was a two-bit gunman, out to get Smith, an' he left friends somewhere hereabouts. But the Injuns got both of 'em, an' they died the same way — kind of hanged with a queer dingus that whistles as it comes. One pretty near got me. Mighty mean weapon, whatever 'tis. If they could throttle its whistle it'd be a dandy."

Roud got his boots emptied of water and his socks wrung out, and pulled them on again. "What gets me is that strange cat girl! She —"

"What we need is a boat," Devlin cut in.

"— had a golden face, of all things! But her body wasn't — I mean — Well —"

Devlin rose. "Get your mind off women, an' let's hike over the rim! My horse is somewhere over there, with a bottle in the saddle pocket."

"I've got a small collapsible canvas boat at my camp," Roud told him. "I didn't use it today, because I didn't know what the river would be like."

Devlin nodded. "Let's get a drink an' start down for your camp before those long-haired river pirates come nosin' back. They know I'm somewhere around on the loose. Maybe we can ease up on 'em in your boat, an' kind o' pay our respects before they can set their whistle dingus on us."

27

"No shooting, please," Roud warned. "I don't want to stir up any trouble."

"Nor me," agreed the Preacher gravely. "I've always found it a good rule to swat trouble before it can up an' bite me!"

It was still dark in the early-morning hours when they made their way down the grassed slopes of Calaveras Valley, and Devlin remarked upon the campfire which he saw burning down near the bottom. "You must've built quite a light before you left camp," he said, "an' forgot to put it out. That's how we get forest fires in this country."

Roud peered down at the flicker. "I didn't," he denied with mild indignation. "I'm no greenhorn when it comes to camping. I always put out my fires."

"Then you've got company waitin' for you," said Devlin, and he thoughtfully slid a hand under his long black coat, his mind on sheriffs and possemen. "Yeah," he added after a moment, "quite a little party. Hm-m-m."

Their descent had been heard, and the Preacher drew his own conclusions from the manner in which the group of men quit the light of the campfire. It was a familiar and suggestive move, not calculated to make for easy trust and assurance of a welcome. Lawmen and outlaws both had that self-preserving habit when in hostile country. The Preacher hallooed a caustic query.

"Anybody home around here?"

According to the lack of any response, nobody was home. Devlin circled the fire, leaving Roud to walk on in if he wanted to. Two men rose from the covering darkness, and then four more. They wheeled slowly, keeping their fronts toward the steady sound of the circling hoofbeats, but unable to pick out the black horse and its somber-garbed rider. When Roud walked into the fire light they glanced at him, inspected him briefly, and turned their searching looks outward into the darkness again. One of them raised an arm, gesturing in the rider.

The Preacher rode in at a walking pace and showed himself. He raked his glance over the six standing men, took estimation of them, and drew the black to a halt, keeping the half dozen visitors between the fire light and himself. They didn't appear to care for that, nor for his looks, for they shifted restlessly on their feet and began to drift apart. Devlin spoke a short greeting.

"Howdy."

A pause, and it was returned. "Howdy."

"Coffee on?" inquired Devlin, his tone remaining flat and clippped.

"Uh-huh. Hot as a high sheriff's neck after an honest election day." It was the usual type of reply, carefully framed to let it be known that the speaker was no friend of the law.

"*Bueno!*" The Preacher swung out of his saddle, stepped past the six close-lipped men to the fire, and helped himself out of the coffeepot. He was aware that they kept their attention upon him, rather than on Roud Connell, and he sensed an element of displeased surprise in their taciturnity. That raised a significant point. They had expected Connell, had been waiting for

29

him to return to his camp. But they had not expected him to return with a companion, and for the moment it posed a problem for them. It was in their eyes.

One of them turned his head slightly, and murmured a word to a tall, white-haired man standing by him. The white-haired man raised his eyebrows, and frankly allowed his expression to show that he was impressed. His clothes had a rakish elegance, their style reminiscent of the card room of a Mississippi River boat, and he had a fine cast of face, marred by a scarred lower lip that tended to drag down one corner of his mouth. His eyes were clear blue, his gaze straight and candid — too candid, Devlin thought, for undiluted honesty. They reminded him of a certain highly successful greenhorn trimmer whom he had once known, who had ambitiously crowded three murders into one night and paid for them the next morning without benefit of trial.

"I believe," said the white-haired man, with a soft voice and courtly manner, "you, suh, are the well-known Preacher Devlin. We're honored — truly honored, suh. In my triflin' way, I also am not without a certain claim to distinction. My name, suh, is Trist — Colonel Montgomery Trist — late of the Mexican *Regimiento Cordada*."

"Also known as Queen-card Monty, I believe, suh," appended the Preacher, spearing a slice of beef from a hot pan. He was acquainted with the name and reputation of the gentlemanly Colonel Trist.

The colonel bowed. "Correct. Cigar? Drink?"

30

He was affable, easy to meet, and wore his courtly charm with a mockingly humorous air when in the company of those who knew him too well to be taken in. The Old South had never known him, but he claimed it as his homeland, and hinted modestly of a great plantation lost with the ill-starred Confederacy. Greenhorns trusted him, lawmen vainly hunted him, and those on his side of the fence recognized him as a genius at finding rich pickings and a deadly devil with any kind of weapon. His presence here stamped the final seal upon Devlin's convictions that there was heavy profit in a jackpot somewhere in the near vicinity. The colonel wouldn't be fooling his time away chasing a legendary treasure cache, if he wasn't sure that such a cache existed.

The Preacher wrinkled his nose. He was beginning to catch a whiff of that jackpot.

CHAPTER
FOUR

It became evident to Devlin that the colonel was making a special effort to cultivate a friendship with him, for one purpose or another. Devlin drank his coffee, ate the beef, accepted a drink and a cigar, and waited for events to shape up.

The colonel took his time about showing his hand, but when he did he was almost disarmingly frank about it. "Mr. Connell" — he inclined his fine white head to Roud, and smiled pleasantly — "I have a great and sincere admiration for the memory of your late lamented father, and a humble respect for his contributions to ethnological knowledge. I am acquainted with his work — some of it, at least — particularly in regard to the tracing of the lost Tewa tribe. You see, suh, I happen to possess your father's notes which he made on that subject."

"What?" Roud came to his feet in a jump. "You've got his papers? Where are they? How did you get hold of them?"

The colonel placed his fingertips delicately together, and gazed pensively at him. "It's quite a long and boring story. I shall spare you the details. Your father, rest his soul, died suddenly. His pack was found floating in the Gato. The finder, an ignorant sheepherder out looking for strays, sold the pack and contents for the price of a bottle. No, not to me. It went through several hands before coming into my possession. Only four or five of the temporary owners understood the notes. Alas, they died like your father!"

"The whistle dingus," said Devlin reflectively.

The colonel flashed his smile. "A very apt name for it, suh. You've heard it, then? So have I. Yes, that was what got them. I . . . ah . . . obtained the notes from a man known as Soldier Smith. He was once a cavalryman, and we old soldiers have a bond among us that —"

"The whistle dingus got him," put in Devlin.

"I'm delighted to know that," responded the colonel blandly. "The runty little twister had memorized the notes, and he hurried on ahead to beat me to it. I sent someone after him. Happen to see my man up there?"

"Yeah. The damn thing got him, too."

"Poor Epp. But we all have to die sometime, don't we?" The colonel shrugged and turned to Roud. "You, suh, are very naturally interested in your father's notes. However, they are not at all complete, unfortunately. But with the results of your own research to add to them, we may very well solve the problem, eh? That's the reason for our visit to your camp. I learned that you were in this region, following in the footsteps of your father, and I took the liberty of tracking you here. Let's form a congenial and gentlemanly partnership, shall we?"

"For what purpose?" asked Roud bluntly. He evidently was not taken in much by the courtly rascal's winning ways.

"For the gold, suh," replied the colonel, just as bluntly. "We'll all go shares in it, if we find it. It will entail a certain amount of . . . ah . . . force, of course, but Mistah Devlin and I and these devoted henchmen of mine can attend to that. Those Indians up there will put up a fight, not a doubt of it. You couldn't get anywhere with them by yourself. You must realize that."

"I didn't come up here for gold, nor for a fight," Roud stated, slowly and with emphasis. "If there's any gold up there, I guess it belongs to the Indians. Anyway, I don't need it."

"Really," the colonel chuckled, politely disbelieving such a declaration of heresy. "Your scruples, suh, are most refreshing in this day and age. Come, now, let's be sensible men. There may be a fortune waiting for all of us up there."

His clear blue eyes took on a glitter, and the sharp edge of the man began to show itself through the velvet of his manners. Greed and danger and cruelty were evident in the set of his scarred mouth, and now he stood for what he was — a hard-bitten and wholly unscrupulous freebooter of fortune.

He stared unblinkingly at Roud. "Young man," he said in a changed and brittle tone, "I've lived too long to believe in scruples where gold is concerned! Quit stalling. We're all here on the same game. We can pitch in and work it out to a finish together. Guns, brains and science — against a pack of long-haired animals from the devil knows where!"

"An' a cat-faced female," remarked Devlin.

The colonel switched his stare to the gun fighter. "*Is* there one? You've seen her? Bloody Christopher! There's a lot to be found up along that lonely old river, eh? Well, my learned young savant, what do you say?"

"I say get to blazes out of my camp!" Roud rapped, and the colonel's five gunmen looked up from the fire where they sat, but their attentive eyes converged on the tall black length of the Preacher.

Colonel Trist, too, scanned Devlin's dark and unreadable face. "And how do you stand on this, suh?" he inquired.

"With science," drawled the Preacher.

The clear blue eyes flickered in the fire light. "So you're going to play for all or nothing, eh? That's a big bet, Mistah Devlin. Other good men have died along the Gato, with the same high-gambling idea! Better think it over. I'd share square, my oath on it."

Devlin shifted his chewed cigar. "Science, suh, must be skeptical," he pronounced, and hooked his thumbs in the broad and double-looped black belts that crossed his waist.

The five gunmen caught their leader's eye. They rose with slow care, picking up their rifles. All five were heavily armed, double-gunned and hung with extra cartridge belts. The colonel bowed, the habit of pseudo-courtesy strong in him, but his finely etched face was blank.

"I trust you will not regret your decision, gentlemen," he breathed, and paced off into the darkness, his gunmen following at heel.

Backing out of the fire light, the Preacher listened for the sound of creaking saddles. He had located the horses as he circled the camp, and knew roughly where they stood tied in a bunch. The sound of saddle leather didn't come, and he began a low, swift warning to Roud. "Get out o' the light, feller! They're —"

A rifle shot cut across his last word, followed by three more, and then a thudding confusion of exploding cartridges. Devlin flung himself down, his hat whipped away by the first shot, and he had his guns flipped out before he hit the ground with his chest. Knowing where the horses were tied, he hammered two shots that way in the hope of catching a man, but only drew forth a whinnying squeal. Then, glimpsing the repeated flashing of a rifle off to his left, he sighted and triggered, and with the second roar of his gun the flashes quit. He hoped that it was Colonel Montgomery Trist that he had hit; but he didn't think so; he knew it wasn't, when the colonel called to somebody to go and hold the horses.

Roud had ducked down when the shooting started, and now he was crawling to the shelter of his piled camp gear. But nothing lethal struck the ground anywhere close to him. It wasn't the young ethnologist that Trist wanted out of the way. It was Preacher Devlin.

Reaching his shelter, Roud dug into a pack. His hand came out with the spindly target pistol that Devlin, when he saw it, figured must have been made and purchased for knocking over medium-sized jackrabbits. It had a barrel about as thick as a bank clerk's pencil, and it was kind of a pitiful weapon to bring up against all those big-calibered repeating rifles and six-guns.

But Roud rested the skeleton tube on top of his gear, took a steady aim, and the target pistol snapped like a firecracker. Surprisingly, someone let out a holler and fell to swearing.

"I got one!" Roud claimed.

"Stung him, anyway. He likely thinks a hornet bit him," commented the Preacher, and his matched pair of heavy man stoppers boomed solidly. "It's a pity that popgun was picked too green an' never grew up, or you might do some good with it. Slide off out o' there, Rowdy, an' cut for the river before they get mad at you. Take your little boat along, if you can. I'll bring up our horses later an' join you. That is, if these hombres don't get too stubborn."

After Roud eased out, lugging a bulky bundle of canvas and cane ribs, Devlin settled down to business. He skirted wide around the camp and shot holes in the coffeepot, which disgorged its liquid contents and discouraged the fire to a sputtering glimmer. Then the Preacher spaced a few more bullets in the direction of the bunched horses. One horse reared up, pawing, and a man skylined himself while running to hold the animal from bolting off. Devlin chopped a shot at him, saw him jump, heard the colonel sounding off again, and then more men were running to the horses.

Saddles creaked under vaulting bodies that landed in them, and hoofs began their pounding on the grassed turf. "First round to you, Mistah Devlin!" came the cool yell of the colonel. "I'll try to do better next time. On my oath I will, suh!"

Devlin grinned faintly, and sent a parting bullet whining after them. To match wits and guns with a tempered sword of a man like the colonel was something of a satisfaction, in its way. The man was no half-hearted gambler. He'd play out the game to its end, with nerve and finesse. This bit of gunplay had been only a preliminary skirmish, an opening salute to the battle to come, and made in the hope of getting in a lucky shot at the start. The hoofbeats drummed off down the valley. Devlin pushed fresh shells into his warm guns, caught up his horse and Roud's roan, and rode for the river.

He found Roud working up toward the mouth of the canyon, where the Rio Del Gato widened out to flow into the valley and join the Calaveras. Roud had the little collapsible boat set up. He mentioned that he had built it himself. "But I forgot to pack along a paddle," he admitted.

Devlin hacked off an oak branch and handed it to him. "There's your paddle, skipper! Let's shove off. We can leave our horses hobbled. They won't stray far, with good grass around."

"This branch will make some noise," Roud pointed out dubiously. "Those Indians might hear us. You know, what I wanted to do was —"

"After all that shootin' racket they'll have their ears cocked big, anyway," growled Devlin. "The noise can't be helped. Trist's more'n likely ridin' to fetch up more reinforcements from his camp, wherever 'tis, so we've got to move fast if we aim to keep ahead of him. Come on, get goin'. An' duck if you happen to hear a funny kind o' whistle. It'll be a flyin' hang rope lookin' for your neck!"

They shoved off, Roud paddling hard with the awkward branch and making slow progress against the current. Devlin helped out by paddling with his hands, and the light and tiny craft took on some speed and veered precariously over to midstream. Devlin didn't have a high opinion of the boat, but he had ridden lots worse things in a pinch. To get first crack at the jackpot, he was ready to swim, if he had to.

Some grayness spread gradually into the dark sky, heralding dawn, and the moon was low, but the night's darkness drained reluctantly from the deep canyon shadows of the Gato. It was very quiet along the river, so hushed that the constant splashing of the oak branch sounded enormously noisy.

"'In the eye of the golden cat that slumbers by the river,'" Devlin quoted reflectively. "What breed of animal would that be?"

"It was intended in a more or less symbolic sense, I imagine," Roud offered. "We'd have to know some of the secrets of old Tewa symbolism, probably, to learn the meaning. May take years. I hope to discover some traces of Tewa rock carvings and picture writings along here, and study them. The chances are small, of course."

He looked around at Devlin, and turned on his engaging grin. "But we scientists must be patient, as well as very skeptical, mustn't we? Yes, and we have to — Say, what's that sound?"

What he heard was a thin, whining cry that raised the echoes, joined them, and caught the vibrating note of the canyon, so that it seemed to be coming from everywhere. The Preacher peered toward the right bank, seeking the source of it, but everything there showed only as a great black wall against the lightening sky. The cry opened on that thin, complaining note, and lengthened, rising swiftly at last to a screeching howl. When it ended, the echoes trailing off and fading behind it, Roud had stopped paddling. The little canvas boat at once lost headway and swung broadside to the stream.

"Cat," muttered the Preacher, and his eyes were narrow. "Make for the bank yonder — fast!"

Roud went to work again with the branch, staring up at the great cliff. "What're you aiming to do, Devlin?"

"Hunt cats!"

The little craft nosed over toward the foot of the cliff. Details began emerging dimly out of the blankness, taking shape as both men drew nearer to the scant strip of shore, and they made out the tenacious scrub brush that grew in clumps along the high ledges. The Preacher sat crouched and watchful, eyes roving, hands spread on his knees. Suddenly he lurched to one side with all his weight, tipping the boat.

40

"Swim for it!" he rasped.

Roud had no option about it. The flimsy little boat promptly keeled over and foundered, unloading him into the river, and he fell in head-first. When he threshed his way right side up and got his head clear, he was gasping and spitting out river water. Devlin was already swimming for the bank with long, powerful strokes.

"Of all the loco things to do!" Roud spluttered angrily, and then a vicious little star flashed high up the canyon wall.

The report filled the canyon with sound and Roud with quick comprehension. Something plopped sullenly in the water near his kicking feet, and while the echoes were rattling back and forth he churned for the shore. The white water that he kicked up behind him made a target, and two more reports rang out. As he scrambled up onto land, one of Devlin's guns whammed twice somewhere ahead and then went quiet.

Roud found himself a rock and got down under the lee of it. "Hey, Devlin, where are you?" he called, and got no answer. The rifle up above fell silent, and the heavy hush crept back in again. The canyon of Rio Del Gato suddenly seemed a very lonely and forbidding place, to a certain wet young ethnologist.

CHAPTER
FIVE

The Preacher inched his creeping course up an erratic ledge that he had located from below, grimly intent upon making connections with the unknown sharpshooter. As he climbed, he could look down onto the wide black ribbon of the river. Now the lightening sky made a dark mirror of the river's smooth surface, and caused a pictured reflection of the opposite cliffs to appear in it.

The somber beauty of the scene drew small appreciation from the Preacher. He was wet, somewhat cold, and not in a good humor. But when specks of movement in the reflection caught his eye, he looked upward and across the canyon, and there on the opposite cliff rode a line of horsemen and pack mules.

Devlin swore under his breath. The colonel and his pack of gunmen had made good time returning, much better time than the slow progress of the little canvas boat. Still, they were on the wrong side, and that was a problem for them. Crossing the canyon and the river might give them plenty of trouble, as long as the cat-squalling shooters on this side maintained their keen watch. The Preacher counted fourteen riders in all, and he could see that they were on the lookout for himself and Roud, from the close way they scanned the river below as they rode the cliff's rim.

And then he heard the low hum of the whistle dingus.

Instinct sent his left arm up as a shield, and he ducked. Something struck his forearm, wound itself in a tight grip around his wrist, and struck again, twice, like a live and active snake. He tried to shake it off. It tangled, but he knew from its limpness that it was not alive. With the thing dangling around his numbed left wrist, he went leaping up the narrow ledge, gray eyes coldly savage and his right hand jerking out a gun.

The rocky face of the canyon wall bulged ahead of him, thrusting out so far that it overhung the river. The ledge ran partly underneath the great bulge and seemingly petered out into space, but Devlin found that it bent and hugged the cliff, continuing onward to still another bend. He made the turn, running in a crouch, and pulled up sharply to flatten himself against the cliff side, catching a blur of movement farther on.

A flash and report exploded along the ledge. The Preacher triggered a fast response, his broad back pressed against the rock, and his gun lined out at arm's length level with his right eye. Somebody sighed audibly, and there was a slight scraping sound and a rustle. Somewhere along there a wounded man was dragging himself back, but the addition of other small noises meant that he had friends within reach.

A blazing volley put an end to those noises, and the canyon roared with magnified reverberations. The angle of fire and the rugged contour of the cliff's face made accurate shooting a matter of lucky chance, but those who guarded the ledge tried to make up for that disadvantage with volume. The tips of red rock protuberances burst here and there into chips and powder, and ricochet bullets droned a many-voiced cacophony. Over on the opposite cliff, the string of riders drew up and quit their saddles.

Devlin back-tracked around the bend, crawling the last few yards on his hands and knees, and took cover from the storm. Through the confused racket he could hear a continual snapping of rifle bolts being jerked open and slammed home, and occasionally an empty shell glinted brassily, sailing outward and downward to the river, ejected fast from a hot and busy breech. They were using Sharps repeaters, he decided, and they either had plenty of ammunition to spend or were mighty reckless with what they did have. Evidently they didn't yet know that he had withdrawn to cover, for they went on shooting like a bunch of Saturday-night drunks.

Devlin rid himself of the thing tangled around his wrist, and worked his fingers to get the numbness out of them. The thing was a braided and heavy cord, he found, with a smooth round stone fastened to each end of it. He thought about Epp Redrick, who had looked as if he had grown two big cars as he tumbled into the arroyo, and he recalled very distinctly how the thing had struck his own forearm twice, painfully, after the first impact. The round stones gave the answer to that aspect of the riddle. When the whirling cord hit and wound itself around its target, the stones slapped hard for the finishing touch. The Preacher sent a glance across at the far cliff. The horses and pack mules were still up there, their backs and heads now tipped with early sunlight, but not Colonel Trist and his gun squad.

Nailed boots scraped on the rocks as the firing lulled, and Roud loomed up, coming along the ledge. "That you, Devlin?" he called. He had his spindly pistol in his hand. "They're crossing the river — the colonel and his crowd — down below the bend! What's all the shooting up here for?"

"For science," grunted the Preacher. "They've been tryin' to excavate into my hide for old relics, an' came damn near doin' it, at that! How far behind you is that mob?"

"Pretty close by now, I guess." Roud rubbed his jaw with the slender barrel of his pistol. He looked down at the river, not too excitedly, and up at the morning sky. "This is getting awkward, isn't it? Too bad we couldn't have made friends with these Indian people. It certainly would come in handy right about now. What's that you've got there?"

The Preacher tossed the stout cord and stones to him. "Just a friendly greetin' they sent me! Take a look at it. Ever see anythin' like it before?"

Roud examined it, and his eyes lighted up with a scientist's zeal. "Why, this is a South American weapon!" he exclaimed, and now he showed some excitement. "It's been used for hundreds of years by the Peruvian Indians, for hunting and war! Peru! You know, they say that when this thing is thrown properly by an expert —"

"Don't worry," Devlin cut in dryly. "They're plenty expert!"

"Why, it's incredible!" Roud was all taken up with his discovery and its significance. "This practically proves —"

"The devil with what it proves," interrupted the Preacher. He was not in a receptive mood for another lecture. "Here comes the colonel an' his guns!"

He drew in his head, a split second before a bullet put a nick in the rock behind him. This place was not so good to hang around in. Too open to view and not much cover to speak of. In a minute the advancing colonel and his shooters would be in a spot where they could get in some handy sniping. Those Indians around the bend were jamming up things badly, blocking the only path of retreat. But then, if those same Indians hadn't been blocked, themselves, they could have operated along the full length of the ridge and kept the colonel from crossing over. The Preacher figured that it was just too bad that he had got himself placed squarely between the two hostile forces. He was out on a mighty high limb.

"You can squat here an' study that fool thing if you feel that way, Rowdy," he growled, "but I reckon I'll take the Injuns for mine!"

"I'm right with you," said Roud at once. "I've simply got to see those Indians now!"

"Better hope they don't see you first," grunted the Preacher. He drew his other gun, took a brief inspection of both, and cocked them. "Well — here goes for science!"

46

Opening his wide mouth, he let out a terrific squall that sounded like a dozen tomcats being stepped on all at the same time. Even Roud winced at the fearful sound and the unexpected suddenness of it. He winced again, catching sight of the dour face as the notorious gun fighter passed him. It was not a benign face at the best of times, and now it was satanic, the slaty eyes oblique and baleful. At such a time, tales told of the veteran long rider became believable.

The Preacher charged around the bend, his black coat tails flying out behind him, and his frayed cigar jutting out as straight as a man-of-war's bowsprit.

What the unearthly sound and sight of the sinister big apparition did to the nerves of the Indians was made evident when for the first few seconds they failed to shoot. They could see Devlin now in the early-morning light; he wasn't just a moving shadow. And they could see his coldly glaring eyes. When they did shoot, it was in a wild, ineffectual way. Roud could understand that, his own nerves being jarred ragged, but what he didn't understand was the way the Preacher veered abruptly aside and vanished.

Several rifles opened up with a solid cracking, back along the ledge where the colonel and his men worked their way. A dark and scantily clad figure with long hair rose like a bent sapling released, a short stone's throw before Roud. It gazed unseeingly at him, closed its dulled eyes, and quietly tumbled off the ledge.

There was some gnarled brush growing close to the cliff wall, and it was from behind this that the Indian had risen. The rifle fire continued behind Roud. Dry twigs and bits of leaves flew from the brush, and there was a hurried rustling as those huddled behind the brush crawled back out of there in rapid retreat.

The voice of the colonel sounded clearly through the canyon, with a cool and almost gay undertone to it. "Watch out you don't drop that young fellow there, my bully boys. We don't want *him* dead!"

Roud jumped for the spot where the Preacher had vanished.

It was a low-roofed cavern into which the Preacher veered, the rear end of it lost in the shadow, although sunlight was now creeping down the face of the canyon wall. He saw a figure running for the back shadow, a slender figure wearing little more than a shirt and an abbreviated skirt, and he swung a gun to bring it down with a shot, but checked his trigger finger at the last instant.

"Halt!" he rapped harshly. "Halt, I say — or do I have to cripple you?"

The slender runner halted in midflight, and turned slowly. Gold shone where the face should have been. The body was youthful, lightly tanned, and looked as lithe and supple as that of a healthy and active young animal. It was the cat girl.

Briefly Devlin scanned the strange, expressionless face of gold. His stare flicked over and beyond it, raking the shadows in the rear. What he saw caused him to dodge and slash upward with a gun. He fired, and while waves of sound rolled and beat along the walls, a rifle could be heard to clatter on the stony floor.

48

"Come on out o' there — right now!" Devlin rapped, and added, "If you're still able."

He had slung his bullet at a dark blob that had shifted almost imperceptibly as he saw it, and he didn't yet know what it was that he might have hit, but the clatter of the fallen rifle was significant enough. Devlin leveled his gun again, this time taking deliberate aim. "I give you two seconds to come out, hombre — an' if you can't *sabe* my lingo, that's your funeral!"

The murky blob had bent over sidewise after the shot. Now it came forward, noiseless in its pacing, and emerged as a sparely built man above medium height, holding both hands to the right side of his body. He wore ragged trousers and a shirt, and leather moccasins, and he had a short beard. His skin was burned a deep brown, and his eyes were coal black, but his beard and untended long hair were a salt and pepper hue.

Roud, coming in on the jump, took one look at the cat girl, another at the bearded man, and gaped. "Why, he — That's a white man!" he blurted.

"I don't need science to know that," returned the Preacher. "Maybe the cat's white, too, when she takes that thing off her head. Looks white from what I can see." He motioned to her. "Take that thing off!"

Two slim, bare arms rose hesitantly. The small hands fumbled at the sides of the golden face, and the face was lifted off. It gave even the Preacher a slightly uncanny feeling to see that trick done. Roud gulped again and stared harder than ever. His scientific fervor

49

appeared to stand the disillusionment of the exposure quite well.

The girl had a wealth of hair that matched the color of the golden mask, and a subdued kind of beauty fashioned to catch and hold the eye of any normal man, even an ethnologist. Her eyes were dark and frightened and she gazed at Roud like a child begging off from punishment. She seemed to feel that the young scientist might be a better prospect for mercy than the forbidding, black-garbed man.

The frightened and appealing gaze had all its own way with Roud, but the Preacher kept his saturnine stare fixed on the bearded white man. "That boogery cat face didn't work so good this time," the gun fighter observed.

The bearded man shrugged, flinched a little at the pain of the movement, and pinched his side with both hands. That side of his shirt was darkening. "I only had a slim hope it might, anyway," he retorted, and he had the brittle coolness of one to whom a tight corner was no novelty. "It worked all right on the Cochuritis and a few others. Kept them scared out. But white men are different. Some white men, that is. You got me in the ribs with that shot, curse you!"

The Preacher nodded. "Yeah. You used her an' that cat face for your scarecrow, huh? An' if that didn't work, you got 'em with a bullet or that Peruvian dingus, while they goggled at her! Who are you?"

"What's the difference? They call me Rebel Jack Latimer where I come from, if that means anything to you — which I doubt. Her name's Shay Winton."

"What's your game here?"

The man who called himself Rebel Jack Latimer shook his head. "I've said all I intend to say. You'll get no more out of me, my trigger-itchy friend!"

The Preacher was disposed to contest that statement, but the rattle of a kicked stone drew his attention back to the more pressing matter of the colonel and his mob. "Pick up that rifle he dropped," he told Roud, and jumped to the mouth of the cavern. "Looks like we make a stand here!"

CHAPTER
SIX

Colonel Trist was a born organizer. He wasn't among the first rank, coming up the ledge. He was somewhere in the rear, telling the others what to do and how to go about it. His voice could be heard, confident, gayly bantering, and his gunmen followed his commands, until one rifle and a pair of large six-guns spat a smoky greeting from up ahead. One man scrambled rearward, minus part of his ear, and another dragged a disabled foot to cover. Then, from the mumble of argument, it appeared probable that the colonel had a slight amount of mutiny on his hands.

Roud grinned at Devlin, and worked a fresh cartridge into the breech of the rifle. "We can hold them off from here till doomsday," he remarked cheerfully.

"I don't care to go hungry that long," said the Preacher, and he looked over his shoulder just in time to see Rebel Jack Latimer taking a run out of the cavern. Latimer had the girl by one hand, and was pulling her along after him.

The Preacher rolled backward and dived across the ground after them. He reached out, hooked an arm around a bare but well-shaped ankle, and brought the girl down in a tumble that fetched a small cry from her. Rebel Jack whirled around. He drew in his lips and seemed about to chance a jump at Devlin, but a long and ugly gun barrel cutting up in line with his beard altered his mind. He dodged, spun on his heel, and was gone faster than any man his age had a right to run.

Roud quit his rifle and came stalking over, scowling like a barroom tough. "Damn you, Devlin! Don't manhandle her like that!" he objected angrily, and assisted the shaken girl to her feet. From the look in the girl's eyes as she was helped up, she was obviously positive that Roud was the only man with any decent feelings around here.

The Preacher eyed them without comment, took a fresh bite on his wrecked cigar, and went back to swapping shots with the colonel's squad. He was halfway tolerant of the vices of his fellowmen, having a fairly complete collection of his own. But this hot spot had been bad enough before the girl took off her golden mask. Now it was developing fresh and potent elements, and Devlin didn't like it. Given a certain stimulus, the most reasonable and tractable man became an illogical idiot full of scrap and noble sentiments. That certain stimulus, Devlin dourly suspected, had virulently attacked a perfectly good ethnologist and ruined him for all rational purposes. It was quite understandable. The girl was pretty, very pretty.

The Preacher took count of his shells, found that they were running dangerously low, and he switched over to the rifle. No use trusting Roud with the rifle just now. The young scientist was a busy and distracted man, tending gently to a grazed knee that belonged to a girl named Shay Winton, and for all he knew the world was a fine place to live in and raise a family.

A tiny fall of dirt sifted down the bold face of the bulging rock above the cavern, and the Preacher jerked up his head to see what caused it. The round muzzle of a rifle was peering down, swinging gently to bear its sight on him. He threw a swift shot up at it, and backed into the mouth of the cavern.

"Some of those hungry gunners have climbed up on top of us," he mentioned, but the remark went unheard, so he kicked Roud to get his attention. Even that passed as a clumsy accident. It took a bullet to penetrate the clouded intelligence of Roud and the girl. The bullet slapped near their feet, fired from overhead. The instinct for self-preservation returned, and they shifted.

"Let me have that rifle!" demanded Roud, seemingly all prepared to dash out and slaughter everybody.

"You're welcome — it's empty," responded the Preacher. "An' I'm runnin' low on shells, too. Young feller, your doomsday sure arrived quick. Five minutes more an' we'll be smoked out!"

He leaned out swiftly and fired upward. Two rifle muzzles were withdrawn from the upper edge of the over-hanging bulge, one with a clang and a jerk. Devlin kept his guns lined on the spot.

"I can make 'em hold their heads in for a while," he said. "Maybe long enough for you two to vamoose off out o' here. But make it fast! You'll be in plain sight when you move out, till you pass that brush clump at the next bend. After that — well, let's hope your goldie head can coax her Injuns to cool off an' be friendly. It's the only chance. I'll follow on when I see my way clear."

Roud hesitated, then nodded. "All right. Come on, Shay. Devlin, if you get stuck here, I'll try to borrow a rifle and shells from the Indians, and I'll come back to give you a hand. Oh — wait. I'd better not take my pistol along, or those Indians won't even begin to trust me. I'll leave it here. They'd never trust an armed man going among them, you know."

"With a load o' such pop toys you still wouldn't be armed!" Devlin opined, and spent one more shot on the round eye of a gun barrel that poked tentatively into sight over the bulging boulder. For the moment he had the shooters up there holding to cover.

He heard a racing patter of feet as Roud and the girl sped out of the cavern, and then a hasty rustle which meant that they had got past the brush clump at the bend of the ledge. Three shots whipped from some distance off, a shade too tardily, and then quietness settled. The men crouching above made no more attempts to shoot down, but they were busy at something up there. They were moving about, whispering, and once one of them choked on a laugh.

"Mistah Devlin!" It was the colonel's pseudo-cultured voice. "Are you still there, suh? Did you notice our pack mules as we came up on the other side? I came up better prepared to handle the situation this time. Quite well equipped to dig, drill, or blast rock —

55

or anything else that needs removing. Permit me to demonstrate. Accept my calling card, suh!"

A tin can came rolling down the boulder, bounced onto the ledge, and settled there. It looked harmless, until the Preacher saw the little curl of smoke and the sputtering bit of fuse stuck into a hole that had been punched into the can.

Devlin took a long stride and booted the can over into the canyon. A bullet immediately pounded splinters from the rock, inches from his toe, and he leaped back to shelter. The five-pound canister of high-test blasting powder boomed like a cannon, halfway down into the canyon, and the colonel chuckled cheerfully behind his cover.

"Splendid, suh! Nice kick. No doubt you were a star rugger player in your college days, what? But you see my point. Too bad we haven't a longer drop for them. A good concussion would set them off nicely. However, we must do the best we can with the conditions at hand, eh? Give me that rope, boys!"

This time no canister rolled down the boulder. Inside the mouth of the low cavern, the Preacher kept sharp vigil. It was as desperate a hole as any he had ever been in. He could see only a short length of the ledge from in here, the section that ran directly past outside, and he knew that it now lay under the short-range threat of the colonel's alert trigger men. They couldn't miss at that range, and from where they lay they could cover all the length of it to the clump of brush and maybe beyond. The Preacher explored the cavern and found it a blind hole. There was no exit out of here, except by way of the one entrance.

Something metallic clanked against rock. A canister swung idly into view at the mouth of the cavern, tied to the end of a rope. Its fuse was short and smoking. There could be no kicking of this one off the ledge, and no time to grab it loose from that held rope and throw.

"*Adios*, suh!" the colonel called down affably. "Drop me a card from hell when you get there, won't you?"

With life teetering on the thin margin of a few seconds, the Preacher wasted no time on debate. But he didn't neglect to snatch up the discarded golden mask on his way out. To die with gold in his hands might not help much in the afterworld, but it went against his principles to leave valuables behind him at any time. One leap took him into the morning sunlight, and the next launched him clear off the ledge. Two hasty shots hammered down at him as he came lunging out of the cavern, and then there was nothing left of him in the range of their eyes to shoot at. He was plunging through space, headfirst, arms out, and still grasping the golden mask.

The colonel swore loudly and surprisedly. "Why, that ornery damned — Back, you fools! That can will blow your heads off, you stick them out there!"

The golden mask was fairly heavy. Its added weight helped to keep the Preacher from turning in midair, and he fell in a straight dive. The deep, smoothly flowing river appeared to rush up to meet him, and when the canister of powder exploded with a thunderous clap behind him he distinctly saw the burst and smoke of it reflected in the water. For that instant he could see the walls of the canyon mirrored beneath him, one side in shadow and the other in sunlight, and the effect was of black and gold.

He hit the river with a mighty splash, shattering its mirrorlike surface, and the force of his high dive carried him clear to the bottom. The gold mask, held straight out before him, struck hard on the rocky bed, sending a shock through his hands and arms. He had to let it go, in order to beat his way up for air. Aching and gasping, he struck out for the nearest point of land directly beneath the cavern and the bulge of rock.

Devlin dragged himself ashore, stumbled up a short slope to the foot of a rocky knoll, and there took cover, breathing hard. Somebody up above was trying to reach him with a busy rifle, but it was purely ambition gone wild, for they could not get a sight of him from up there. The Preacher paid no heed to the hopeful shooting. He wasn't interested right now in making a duel of it. He stretched out in his rocky hollow and relaxed in the warm sunshine. Enough was enough. Let them try that same dive, if they were so almighty ambitious.

The firing ended, but soon opened up again in steadier style a little farther on. Trist and his scrappers had evidently pushed on past the cavern to establish contact with the Indians, and another fight was on.

The Preacher got his breath back, sat up, and cocked a speculative eye over the rocky knoll where he rested. He had seen it as he fell, mirrored in the river, and it had caught his eye because it had looked like a hill of glittering gold in the sunlight. But it wasn't gold. Devlin dug the point of his knife into the rock, testing it without any hopeful expectancy. Myriad flecks of iron pyrites embedded in it gave the whole knoll that alluring sparkle when the sun struck it at an angle. Fool's gold. It was like a symbol of futility. He listened to the fight going on above. Bullets were singing out a lively chorus up there. Once Devlin heard the colonel give out a shout in his unmistakable voice and optimistic fashion.

"We've got 'em, boys! We've got 'em! Give 'em hell!"

The Preacher squinted upward, but there wasn't much he could see from down here, until he sighted a man in ragged trousers and shirt attempting to climb down the face of the canyon wall. Rebel Jack, it seemed, was desperately seeking a way out of one more tight corner, and he had the nerve to try any risky course.

A head with a big Texas hat on it bobbed into view with a rifle. Devlin drew and took a shot at it, but the range was tricky and he had to get his bullet off fast. Big Hat drew back hurriedly, edged up at another spot, and let fly with a snap shot. Somebody else joined him, and bullets began digging the iron pyrites out of the knoll. Rebel Jack continued his slow and laborious descent, but he got to a sheer drop off, and there he was stopped.

Devlin got off a shot that either hit or discouraged Big Hat, for he didn't show up any more. But his partner stuck to it and went on sniping, occasionally sending a blind one down at Rebel Jack on his precarious perch. For a few minutes it was a duel, and then the man with the rifle quit at about the same time that the Preacher ran out of shells.

The Preacher sent a hail up at the stalled and clinging man. "Roost or fly, Rebel. Make up your mind!"

Rebel Jack took the hint. He straightened up and made his jump. He turned end over end, falling, but he hit the river feet first and went under, and the Preacher went splashing in after him. There wasn't much sense left in Rebel Jack when the Preacher hauled him ashore to cover, and it looked likely that he was badly done up, what with his wound and all. But he was a tough-fibered kind of man, and soon he was sitting up and swearing to himself.

"Looks to me like you ran out on the fight, Rebel," remarked the Preacher.

Latimer nodded. He was haggard, and he appeared a lot older now than he had awhile ago. "You might say I did," he agreed heavily. "The game's blown up! My Indians turned against me at last. They're taking a bad beating, and they blame me for it. They've been pepper-tempered for a long time now, and this was the final stinger that set them off. I'm all finished." He lay down again, grimacing. "Oh, well, a man's bound to lose out sometime, and I've turned many a good trick in my day. Thanks for pulling me out of the river. I doubt if I could have made it."

" 'In the eye of the golden cat that slumbers by the river,' " quoted the Preacher. "No such animal, huh?"

Rebel Jack glanced at him, but showed little surprise. "So you know that much, do you? Well, I've thrown away six years, searching this cursed canyon from end to end, the whole twenty miles of it. The nearest thing to gold I've ever found in it is this rock hill we're sitting under. It isn't gold, and it's nothing like a cat! Even so, I've dug and clawed into it wherever I could, particularly here in this hollow. Found nothing. It's solid rock all through. You couldn't hide a dollar in it that a boardinghouse keeper couldn't find."

"What about that gold mask?"

Rebel Jack laughed shortly. "I brought that in with me. Got it down in Peru — that's where I first heard about the Tewa treasure. Don't ask me how the rumor got way down there. I don't know. Maybe some Tewa Indians went south down the old Turquoise Trail. Would've taken them years, but they did things like that in those old days. Anyway, I stumbled on the story while exploring the Ucayli back country for diamonds. The people there are Indians, pretty much like the Pueblo Indians here in New Mexico, some of them. I lived with a tribe for a year, till their headman took a dislike to me, and then I tried to stir up a revolt against him."

He uttered his short, dry laugh again. "I've mixed in all kinds of revolutions for many years," he explained. "Man, the ups and downs I've had, south of the Rio! But I fell short with those Ucayli Indians. The headman won, and I had to get out on the run. Those who sided with me had to bolt, too, or stay and die. Bad eggs, though, all of them. I never trusted them. Renegades, like me. We stole that gold mask, along with other stuff the headman used in ceremonies. It's not so old, but I guess the design is. There's still gold in that Ucayli back country, if a man could get it."

"Where'd that girl come from?" queried the Preacher.

"Daughter of Gunboat Johnny Winton," Rebel Jack said shortly. "Gunboat was a soldier of fortune, like me, and I met him in Lima. I put the proposition up to him, and he threw in with me. He was always ready for anything. But he got into a fight with a crazy Dutchman who stabbed him dead, a week after we left Lima. I couldn't turn his kid adrift, so I brought her along with me. I smuggled my Ucayli Indians in by way of Mexico, and brought them here to help me hunt for that Tewa stuff. We scared the Cochuritis into selling us supplies regularly and keeping their mouths shut."

"Your Ucaylis did a bit o' murder here an' there, too," remarked the Preacher.

Rebel Jack gestured casually. "You know how it is with such benighted devils. You tell them to keep strangers out, and they take it to mean kill them. No use trying to stop them, and it did help to keep this canyon private. I bought a stack of rifles and showed them how to shoot. When you're in a thing, you might as well go in all the way. Cutting the cat face on the hands of killed men was their own idea, though — like taking a scalp."

He was cold-blooded about it, being a man who had dealt so long with violence, that death to him was a commonplace matter.

"Sounds like they're puttin' up quite a fight," the Preacher said, with an upward glance.

"Oh, they'll fight, all right," Rebel Jack averred, "but they're whipped. Shay was with them, last I saw, and that young fellow. The Ucaylis didn't turn against Shay. They're fond of her, in their queer way. But they'd like to rip me into little bits for getting them into this mess! They're holed up in some caves that we lived in, and they can't retreat any farther."

CHAPTER
SEVEN

The firing steadied, with long intervals between shots. Evidently the confident colonel had been temporarily stalled in his storming tactics, and the battle had resolved itself into a deadly sniping contest that might last all day.

"I hope your Injuns have plenty shells," Devlin said. "Usin' Sharps, aren't they? Was that why you didn't take that Ballard rifle of Soldier Smith's?"

"The knotty little guy?" Rebel Jack nodded. "Our shells didn't fit that gun, and he'd fired off everything. We went back later and took him away, and the other fellow, too."

"I saw you."

"You did? We buried them up the canyon. I always made the red devils bury their catch, in case the law ever got curious about things and came up to look around." Rebel Jack stared coolly at the Preacher. "Well, now you know what's what. But if I'm any judge, you're as wide off the law as I am, so I reckon you won't be doing much about it! As for me, I'm going to vamoose out of this cursed canyon and strike south for good old Mexico!" He rose shakily and peered up the cliff.

The Preacher also rose. "What about that girl?"

"Shay? What about her?" Rebel Jack spread his hands. "Nothing I can do. I'm sorry about her, sure. She's a good kid and she's had a tough life. But what the hell? I took care of her while I could, and I was decent to her. The game's all blown up now, though, and I've got to think about my own skin. When a man's done his best and still it's not good enough, all he can do is forget it. I never did believe in looking back. You see too many ghosts that way!"

His callous philosophy penetrated even the Preacher's toughened conscience. The gun fighter laid a heavy hand on him and swung him around. He motioned curtly across the river. "That's the way we're goin' — not south! See those horses up there? We're goin' to cross this river down below the bend, hike up that arroyo on the other side, help ourselves to horses an' ropes — an' stampede the rest. We're goin' to ride around an' come up over this cliff. Then we'll see if we can't get down to the ledge with those ropes, an' horn in somehow on the colonel's party!"

Rebel Jack eyed him. "You can't climb or get a horse over this canyon without going way down into the Calaveras Valley and crossing there at the ford, twenty-odd miles from here," he stated positively. "Then, after you cross, you've got Satan's own piece of country to get all snarled up in on the other side, if you turn west. I know. I've scouted it. It'd take all day and some more to work around up to the top of this cliff — and then what in blazes could be done against that gun crowd? Forget it!"

"Get a move on!" commanded the Preacher, and his tone did not encourage further argument. "I don't quit easy. An' don't you try another slide out on me, or I'll chop you into Peruvian hash!"

Rebel Jack swore resignedly, surrendering to the inevitable and recognizing the chill promise of slaughter when he met it. He was not the only dealer in violence around here. "The route will take us nearly in sight of the Cochuriti pueblo," he grumbled.

"Good," said the Preacher. "Maybe I can pick up some shells there. I'm clear out."

He prodded Rebel Jack, and they crept from cover. Together the two veteran campaigners of many dark trails began working their way down beyond the blind bend.

The day was gone and evening had deepened to nightfall when the two horses came to a halt, blew long sighs, and stretched their necks to explore for grass. Everything was quiet, not a sound coming up from the canyon of the Rio Del Gato below.

"Well, here we are," muttered Rebel Jack Latimer, and he staggered when he dismounted. "We're way too late, as I knew we'd be. It's finished and done. Satisfied?" He leaned against his horse, his chin on his chest. "I'm all in."

The Preacher waved him quiet, and listened for sounds not only in the canyon but in other directions. In Cochuriti pueblo, he and Rebel Jack had met with luck that was none too good. There was a strong chance that word of their visit might have reached the ears of a certain sheriffs posse that had been riding in circles.

The proprietor of the Cochuriti trading post had been gruff and conservative, but not unfriendly, until a lean, high-nosed man entered and caught his eye. The proprietor was middle-aged, and had the look of a worn-out old cowhand who had turned to trade for his living. After catching the weighted glance of the high-nosed man, he looked away.

"Sorry, gents," he said. "I got no shells for sale."

The Preacher let his gaze drift over the high-nosed man, who wore a new gun and belt, and he placed him as a part-time deputy attached to the Indian Agency, here on a routine visit. The fellow had that extra-brisk manner of petty authority, and he was young enough to be crazy brave. It would take a few more years of experience to instill wisdom and discretion into him. The Preacher turned back again to the counter.

"Don't you keep shells in stock?" he queried.

"I gen'rally do," admitted the proprietor, "but I've run out." Being more or less under the control of the Indian Agency, he had to be careful. His faded eyes met those of the deputy, and he added formally: "Anythin' else I could sell you?"

The deputy moved from the open doorway to a stack of Navaho blankets, and the Preacher was aware that he was being scrutinized — his clothes, his face, his whole appearance. The examination passed on to Rebel Jack, to his ragged attire and bloodstains. The deputy shifted farther behind the stack of blankets, and a tightness spread over his face. A showdown was building up.

"How much for that bridle?" inquired the Preacher, and lounged around behind the counter to take a closer look at it. He stooped. "Well — here's somethin' I'll buy."

The proprietor had a gun under the cash drawer. He said nothing as the Preacher picked it up and broke it open, and the deputy couldn't see what was going on. There were only two shells in the gun. The Preacher, still stooping, transferred them to one of his own guns so quickly that it looked like jugglery. With his gun in his hand, he straightened up. He looked over the counter at the deputy.

"His shells just fit my iron," he said. "Lucky, huh?"

The deputy didn't think it so lucky, and his expression said so. For a moment he did nothing, looking at the Preacher's gun. Finally he came out from behind the blankets, paced stiff-legged across the floor, and left. Very soon after, a horse clattered out of the pueblo at a fast run.

Devlin slapped a silver dollar on the counter. "For the shells. You'll never make a bigger profit."

"Maybe they're worth that to you," said the proprietor, and picked up the dollar. He stood at his door, squinting after the two outlaws when they rode out.

The Preacher trod carefully to the rim of the canyon, leaving Rebel Jack leaning against his horse. Here the rim sloped downward for a short distance before dropping away to form the steep wall. Something that was not a rock lay halfway down the curving slope, and the Preacher paused at sight of it. He made it out to be a man, a dark-skinned man, nearly naked, and after some inspection he decided that it lay too still to be a live one.

He sent a low call to Rebel Jack, and eased himself down the slope. The Indian was dead, had been dead only a little while, from the trace of warmth still left in the body. He was long-haired, short and skinny, his loincloth and moccasins worn ragged. There was an empty cartridge belt around his waist, and his bare back was rough with dried blood. The Preacher slung the body over his back and retraced his way.

Sitting wearily on the ground, Rebel Jack watched Devlin come up over the rim with the dead Indian and set the body down. He moved over to the corpse and looked woodenly at it. He ran a hand around the cartridge belt, and nodded.

"Shot off all his shells. These Ucaylis never would learn to save on ammunition or anything else. Just blazed away and no idea when to quit. Then he started climbing, but they got him in the back, and he died where you found him. Maybe some of the others tried the same way out. Maybe some of them made it. They climb like monkeys when they have to."

He looked about him into the darkness, and seemed to shrink into himself. "I'd hate to run into any of them, if they're on the loose up here! When those devils turn against you they keep only one idea in their heads, and that's to kill you. They're all burned out on Rebel Jack, believe me! They figure I'm bad luck to them. Maybe they're right, but I don't want to die for it.

They're bitter homesick, too. So am I — homesick for any place a long way from here!"

"Your mind's all full o' Rebel Jack's troubles, ain't it?" said the Preacher.

"It sure is," retorted the soldier of fortune. "Why shouldn't it be?"

Devlin didn't argue that point. He got one of the ropes that he'd taken from the colonel's equipment, tied an end to a blackjack pine, and lowered himself down the slope to the drop off. In a minute he clambered back up, and joined two more ropes. "I think I see a light down there," he said. "Can't tell exactly, with those big shoulder rocks in the way, but it 'pears to come from the ledge. I'm goin' down to take a look around. You stand watch."

"What'll I do if anything crops up?"

"Pray out loud!" grunted Devlin, and he went down the rope while Rebel Jack sat and watched him go.

After he passed the slope and the first rocky knob, Devlin knew he'd been right about the light. It fanned out in two beams over part of the ledge, as though from doorways hidden from him, and as he descended hand over hand down the rope he detected a murmur of voices. The caves of which Rebel Jack had spoken lay beneath him, off to one side, and the light shone from two of them. He lowered himself onto the long bulge overhanging the ledge, and when he got to the outer edge of that he saw the lighted mouths of the caves below to his right.

The joined lengths of rope ended here, and Devlin let it go. To climb down the side of the long bulge to the ledge could be managed handily enough, but the need for silence made it a ticklish business. The deep canyon magnified and echoed every sound, and there was no wind to cover it up. He began the short descent, and paused, all his lively senses humming, as a half-finished cry broke through the night.

Terror and hopelessness were in that cry, and it was cut off before it got well started. The muffled murmur of voices ceased in the cave below. Some stones rattled, and the Preacher looked up.

Something else was falling, besides stones — an object whose outline twisted and bent grotesquely against the night sky, ragged trousers and shirt flapping, and two round balls dangling and dancing around its neck. It struck rock, rolled, fell off, and then tumbled from one protuberance to another like a man falling down a mammoth flight of stairs. The long and outward-thrusting shoulder of the bulge was its last obstacle. It hit the edge within yards of the Preacher, bounced off, and finally raised a splash as it dropped into the Gato.

And that, the Preacher decided grimly, was the end of Rebel Jack Latimer, revolutionist and shady soldier of fortune, who hadn't believed in looking backward for fear he'd see too many ghosts. Some prowling and vengeful Ucayli survivor had got him — and at the most inconvenient time, as far as the Preacher was concerned.

CHAPTER
EIGHT

They were coming out, the colonel and his men, and they extinguished their light before they came. It left only the weaker light of the other cave, and they avoided that. The Preacher lay flat along the top of the bulge, hoped that the rope would not be noticed, and silently bedamned the fact that he had only two shells for his guns.

He heard Trist say with a laugh: "Must have been one of the long-haired monkeys who got away. Got stuck up there and finally slipped off, I guess. How's our wrathful young scientist and the charmer getting on? Take a look, Lang."

"Shall I put out their light?"

"No. I'll want to talk with them when we finish eating."

Boots clumped off, returned. "They're all right. He's just as perky, an' she's pretty as ever."

"Never mind how pretty she is. I'll be the judge of that!"

They trooped back into the larger cave, and the light came on again in there. The Preacher waited awhile, and slid carefully down to the ledge. Nobody was on watch, and the smaller cave was the one nearer him. He crept to it, peered in, and after a pause entered, taking with him a lurking premonition that he might be running his head into a trap.

Neither Roud nor the girl noticed him enter. They sat back to back on the floor, their wrists roped together, and a candle burning. When Roud did look up and see the somber figure moving like a specter in the candlelight, he gave a violent start. He had a bruise on his forehead and his shirt was in shreds. His start caught the girl's notice. She looked around, and she, too, gave a jump.

"Great guns, Devlin, how did you get here?" Roud breathed. "They're watching for you to come back. Who fell?"

"Rebel Jack," murmured the Preacher. "I came down slower." He decided against putting out the candle. Drawing his knife, he cut the cords from the prisoners' wrists. "The rope I came down on is still there, an' that's our route out. Easy now!"

Roud rose stiffly, and helped Shay to her feet. Their muscles were cramped, making them fumbling and awkward in their movements. The Preacher, leading the way out, stopped short, blocking them. His eyes stilled and went oblique. The cave's entrance was a rough oval, but one side of it jutted inward, which cast a shadow across the ledge. He could swear that the shadow had moved. He watched, and its outline changed slightly, and now he knew that his premonition had been correct.

He shoved Roud and Shay rearward, kicked out the lighted candle, and stood motionless, a gun in his fist and two shells in the gun.

A chuckle sounded outside. "You're a wary bird, Mistah Devlin! But I saw that rope. Was it Jack Latimer who took the long tumble? Too bad. Well, suh, what about coming out?"

"What about you comin' in?"

"Ah, no. Somebody might get hurt in the dark. I don't want Connell or the girl to get killed, y'know. But if they'll come out, some of us may oblige you and come in."

"They're stayin' here! You've got a problem, Trist."

The colonel chuckled again. "That's no problem. Boys, let's have a fire. A nice big fire to warm their hearts! Then they'll *all* come out!"

The Preacher sat on his heels, gun between his knees, and listened to activity outside. He didn't need to be told what was coming, but he did need inspiration as to how to circumvent it. This cave was small. It wouldn't take much of a fire to turn it into a Pueblo baking oven. In the reflected light that shone from the other cave, he watched a pile of dry brush being shoved with a long branch into the entrance. The man manipulating the branch got careless and exposed a hand. Tilting his gun, Devlin fired in a flash. The branch fell, the worker howled, and the colonel laughed.

"Nice shot, suh. He'll never write his name with that hand, but then he never could, so what's the odds? He'll learn to be more careful when he pokes around a wolf trap! Can I give you a light for your cigar, suh?"

A match scraped, and its flame described an arc as it was tossed onto the piled brush. It fell between twigs

74

and came to rest on two of them. The Preacher decided in favor of spending his last shell. He took aim, fired, and the flame was wiped out.

"Egad, how the man shoots!" complimented the colonel. "Let's see what he can do with these."

This time a bunch of lighted matches was scattered into the brush, and the Preacher put away his empty gun. The fire took hold at several points, and in a minute the whole pile was ablaze. Smoke poured into the cave, the heated air swirling it against the low roof. Devlin tore off his coat and began fanning, trying to beat up an adverse draft, but he had to quit and flatten down when a gun thudded outside.

"Get down!" he threw at Roud and Shay.

The heat grew increasingly fierce inside the cave and smoke made breathing a torture.

"Are y'all comfortable in there?" called the colonel. "Boys, throw some more brush on that fire. We don't want our friends to catch cold!"

Roud, his eyes streaming, came dragging over to the Preacher. "Shay can't bear it any longer!" he choked. "We've got to give up!"

"Yeah," the Preacher growled, and raised his voice to a shout. "All right, Trist. You win!"

"I thought so!" responded the colonel brightly. "Jump to it, boys. They want out!"

The fire was swept with long branches off the ledge into the river. Roud took Shay's arm and they staggered blindly through the smoke for the exit. The Preacher brought up the rear, thirstier than he'd been in a long time. Clean air greeted them outside, and they gasped it in. The gunmen stood ranged on both sides of the entrance, ready to shoot.

The colonel had a canteen ready. He handed it to Shay, with a bow, and gave Roud a shove. "Take them away, boys!"

Then he turned to the Preacher, holding a gun cocked and leveled at him. "Y'know, I half expected you to come out shooting. Used up all your nerve?"

"No — just my shells." The Preacher took his guns out slowly, showed the empty chambers, and thrust them back again.

Trist smiled. "Well, well, if we'd only known that! Oblige me by stepping close to the edge."

"Why?"

"Because, suh, we've had enough mess to clean up around here, and Mistah Devlin is about to step out of my life — with a bullet in him! Come, let's not waste more time. I've got things to do. I've got to work on Connell and the girl, and persuade them to talk. The shooting of you, suh, will give me as much pleasure as the task ahead of me!"

"You flatter me," murmured the Preacher. He stuck his hands in his empty belts, and he didn't shift. "Let me put you straight an' save you that work. Connell can't tell you much, an' the girl knows less. Nothin' you do to them can put you any nearer to that Tewa cache than you are right now!"

The colonel lost some of his assurance. His eyes took on their hungry glitter. "They *must* know! Connell has done years of research. Jack Latimer —"

"Jack Latimer found nothin'," cut in the Preacher. "He was ready to quit. Connell's knowledge can be boiled down to one sentence: 'In the eye of the golden cat that slumbers by the river.' Jack Latimer knew that much. It didn't help him, an' he searched for six years."

"Liar!" the colonel snarled, but his gush of rage was evidence that his confidence was shaken. "By Christopher, I'll have the pleasure of killing you, anyway, if I never find the cache!"

"You'll never find it if you kill me, that's sure," the Preacher agreed, and watched to see the significance of his words sink in. He was a gambler, and now he was gambling on his last card, but from his casual arrogance he could have been holding aces and the joker.

The colonel's scarred mouth twitched. "What do you mean?" he almost whispered. "You mean — *you* know where it is?"

Devlin shrugged one big shoulder and gazed idly across the dark canyon. "I'm mighty dry. Throat's like a rasp. Sure, I know. Would I have come back here if I didn't? What about a drink?"

The colonel stared at him for a long time. He, too, was a gambler, not slow to make sudden decisions and change his bets. He finally nodded toward the big cave. "Drinks in there. I'm behind you, so no tricks!"

In the lighted cave the Preacher chose a bottle and drank. The gun group eyed him and their leader. Roud and Shay looked at him hopefully, wondering.

"How about a deal, Trist?" the Preacher said quietly.

"Sure," answered the colonel softly — and too promptly. "Shares. Fifty-fifty."

77

"An' those two there?"

"They're yours. I'll turn them loose. My oath on it."

Devlin helped himself to cigars. "I'll take you to the cache first thing in the mornin'. Bring your tools an' stuff. Need a boat, too."

"Got one," spoke up one of the men. "We found that Injun canoe hid down the river."

Devlin nodded. "*Bueno*. Let's get some sleep."

An hour later, the Preacher opened one eye. Roud lay near him, and Shay was curled up in a borrowed blanket behind them. Four of the men sat awake by the lighted lamp, rifles close at hand. Devlin stretched a leg experimentally. All four men turned wakeful eyes sharply to him, and dropped hands to their rifles. There would be no chance for tricks in this cave tonight.

The Preacher composed himself for sleep, pushing from his mind the prospect of a morning thorny with problems.

They waited on a stretch of the lower bank at the bottom of the canyon, across from the ledge, and the sun was coming up. The gunmen moved restlessly, muttering among themselves. Roud and Shay stood side by side, hopeless, saying nothing. Devlin, with a fresh cigar to chew on, gazed absent-mindedly at the river as it flowed past at his feet.

The colonel's stretched patience snapped. "Damn you, Devlin, you're stalling!" he rapped. "It's light enough now to see anything. You don't know where that cache is, any more than I do!"

78

The Preacher brought his faraway gaze from the river. "Take it easy. Goin' off half-cocked will get you nothin'. Wait awhile. That golden cat is a shy critter, an' has to be caught at the right time."

The minutes dragged by, and a murderous mood simmered among the gunmen. Some of them began cursing in low, flat tones, stroking their holsters and glaring at the Preacher's broad back. Roud and Shay drew closer to the gun fighter, and sat down by him.

"It's no use, Devlin!" Roud whispered. "You've gone the limit. There's no golden cat in this canyon, and you know it!"

The Preacher merely glanced broodingly at him, and went on chewing his cigar. The sunlight moved down the tall face of the great cliff opposite, touched the bottom, and spread out over the strip of shore line. A click behind him brought Devlin's head around, and he looked into the muzzle of the colonel's cocked pistol.

Trist spoke in a strangled voice. "You've been stringing me! I'm going to blow your —"

"Look across the river," said the Preacher. "Look hard — an' you'll see that cat!"

They all looked, their eyes eager to find what they sought. A full minute passed, and somebody began cursing again in a high, strained tone. "There ain't no damn cat, blast him."

"Look again," said the Preacher. "Turn your thick heads over sidewise an' look again." He turned his own head over. "Like this. Like you're lyin' down. That knoll yonder. Look at it. Look at its reflection in the river, an' then tell me you see no cat!"

They did as he said. Roud did, too, and Shay. And there was the cat — the head of a great golden cat, lying sidewise like their own. The knoll, shining with fool's gold, had looked like nothing, in itself. The hollow place in it, where the Preacher had taken cover, and all the general shape of it, had not even remotely resembled anything like a cat. But now, with the sun slanting on it, casting shadows and reflecting it in the river, it was different. The knoll and its reflection, seen together as a whole, formed the illusion of a perfect head — the head of a golden cat with pointed ears, blunt nose and slanted eyes.

There was silence, broken only by hard breathing. The Preacher righted his head and looked around at the colonel. "Well, there it is. What more d'you want?"

The colonel raised a hand that was not quite steady, and pointed at the knoll. "That little hollow spot. 'In the eye of the golden cat — ' That's it! That's where we dig! Right in the eye!"

He laughed aloud, his bright eyes glittering. He had got back his cool, mocking assurance. "Thank you kindly, Mistah Devlin! I'll enjoy showing you everything we dig out of there — and I'll enjoy killing you while your mouth waters at the sight of the loot! Lang, keep a gun on him. Watch Connell, too. He may still come in useful."

Devlin nodded without change of countenance. "I didn't expect anythin' different," he allowed. "A skunk's still a skunk, even after he's deodorized an' perfumed! But what about that girl?"

"She, suh, goes with the rest of the loot!" stated the colonel, and then Roud jumped at him.

Roud didn't get far. Lang, a leathery length of bone and muscle, leaped lightly and tripped him, tapping him with a gun butt as he fell. Casually, the gunman kicked him when he tried to struggle up. "Stay there, greenhorn! All right, colonel, I'll watch 'em — an' I sure hope the Preacher tries a move!"

The colonel led the way to the canoe, and it was something of a race between him and his squad. Gold fever had gripped all of them. They piled into the canoe, clambering over the digging equipment that had been loaded into it, and nearly swamped the craft. Some of them grabbed up the crude paddles and flailed the water. The colonel, as usual, commandeered the best seat for himself, on the wooden box of canisters in the stern. From there, as the canoe nosed for the opposite bank, he turned and waved a hand.

"'Thus did the good ship *Argonaut* sail for the Golden Fleece,'" he recited gayly. "'The mariners at their tasks did toil — '"

"A hell of a navy," said the Preacher.

The canoe gained headway despite the inexpert paddling, and the Preacher sat and watched it. He glanced toward Roud and saw that Shay was with him, and Lang standing over them and grinning. Roud caught Devlin's eye and started to say something, but the Preacher spoke first. "Science should be prepared," he murmured, and Roud followed his glance to Lang's legs.

The colonel was still reciting.

"'Down the paths of the ocean gods the sturdy bark — '"

Devlin called softly: "*Adios*, Colonel!"

The poetry ended. Trist looked around, and his eyes froze on the Preacher's right hand. He saw the hand come out of the Preacher's high boot leg with a spindly little target pistol that was an insult to pull on any man. But he saw where the little pistol was pointing. He dug for his gun and let out a shout.

"Lang! He's —"

The little pistol popped at the same time that Roud flung himself at Lang's legs, but it was a pop that was immediately followed by a roaring blast that shook loose rocks down the canyon walls. The box of powder canisters, pierced by the little bullet, vanished in a pillar of smoke and a high flash of flame, and with it the colonel and half the canoe. The air seemed full of broken picks and spades, and echoes kept booming up and down the canyon.

The Preacher ran to where he'd last seen Lang, and found both Roud and Shay trying to handle him. He hit Lang with the little pistol and broke the butt, but that wasn't enough, so he followed up with a fist, and the gunman quit.

Roud and Devlin rose and stood together, looking at the river. A bit of the canoe floated downstream, and here and there a man pawed dazedly for the far bank. The explosion had been deafening, but it came to the Preacher that he could hear far-off voices yelling somewhere. He looked around, and finally up. Atop the opposite high cliff were horses and men. The men were trying to find a way down, but Colonel Trist's squad had yanked the rope down last night.

The Preacher prodded Roud and Shay. "Let's go. I don't like this place any more!"

He led them up the arroyo. The colonel's horses were back in the same place, now tethered. The Preacher hankered for a saddle under him and a westerly direction out of New Mexico, with all that law up yonder trying to get intimate with him. His own black mount was down in the Calaveras, and he'd have to make smart time to find it and light out before that sheriff's posse got there on the long way around.

Roud and Shay had to work hard to keep up with him, going up the arroyo. "How in the world did you know about that cat's head?" Roud asked.

"Saw it just before I hit the river, when I took that header off the ledge," answered the Preacher shortly. "It only shows up for a few minutes, when the sun's right and the river's smooth. I thought I'd found the cache. Later on, Rebel Jack told me he'd already dug into that hollow spot an' found nothin'."

"Then that's not the cat after all, eh?"

They reached the horses, and saddled three. "Yeah, that's the cat, all right," the Preacher admitted after a pause. "But Trist was goin' for the wrong eye. I knew he would."

"But there's only one eye?"

"What about the one that's reflected in the river?" the Preacher suggested. "That river's got a hard-rock bed. There's a big hard-rock shelf right under where that eye's reflected, in front of the knoll, an' it forms a kind o' natural riffle that holds anythin' from bein' washed on downstream."

"How do you know that? It's deep there."

"It sure is. Hell, that's where I went under when I dived. I couldn't see much, an' I needed air, but I did see a few articles that looked promisin', half buried in the rocks an' gravel."

They mounted the horses and set off. "I'm going to organize a research expedition and explore that spot!" Roud vowed eagerly. "Why, the scientific value of those Tewa relics would be —"

"You an' your science!" growled the Preacher. "You'll put 'em in a museum, huh?"

"Naturally," Roud agreed. "After that, I'm certainly going to head an expedition into Peru. It's very possible that there's a distinct tribal connection between those Ucayli Indians and the lost Tewas. Er . . . would you go with me, Shay?"

"Of course, Roud," the girl said simply. "Anywhere."

"That," said the Preacher dryly, "ought to be an interestin' scientific experiment!"

They laughed, their color high. "If my investigations lead to anything, you ought to get some of the official credit, Devlin," Roud remarked.

"Never mind the credit. I can't use that. Rowdy, when you go fishin' around in the river you'll find that gold mask. I dropped it in there. I figure it ought to be mine — just as a souvenir o' science."

"Right," Roud conceded. "I'll hold it for you till you write and let me know where to send it to you." His face glowed, like Shay's. They exchanged a happy smile.

84

"Why, Shay, we've got a lifetime of the best work in the world laid out for us!"

The Preacher let his eyes rest on the glowing, golden-haired girl. "You sure have, young feller, you sure have! Listen, you two can dawdle, but I'm in a little hurry, myself." He kicked his horse and it stretched out for a long lope. "S'long — an' if you meet that posse, tell 'em I couldn't wait! I got some scientific poker to tend to in Tombstone!"

PART TWO

CHAPTER
ONE

The Brindle Kid was in his glory. He stood before the Concordia Saloon on Rainbow's main street, hands on his hips and hat cuffed to the back of his sleek yellow head, a young gun grandee of perky pride for all the town to see.

"We sure got him — Stamp an' Blackfoot an' me!" he crowed.

He wagged a finger at a magnificent black horse tied to the Concordia hitch rack. The animal was dusty from recent travel. "Brothers, I'm here to tell you he'll never ride that beaut again!"

The Concordia crowd listened attentively. Many of the listeners were connoisseurs of violence. Being such, they had critical skepticism for those who talked too much. But in this case the deed went with the word, and they knew it. The Brindle Kid was no false alarm, for all his flash and brag. His darting young eyes, shallow as mirrors, could go bright with laughter while he pulled the trigger on a man too slow or unprepared to shade him. His face, with its pockmarks, pointed chin and big ears, was a caricature of youth. He was the product of a tough and varied environment that had burned into him a viperish sense of humor. A gun butt was his calculus in simple arithmetic, and he stood high in the service of Stampede Solary, a discriminating picker of useful hirelings.

"We was toughin' it through that sand storm this mornin', comin' back from Aguila, when we saw him," said the Kid and continued his story.

Meantime, the town of Rainbow went on about its business. Once, not so long ago, it had been a cow town, comfortably shabby, but prosperity had come like an explosion and changed all that. Placer gold had been discovered along Contention Creek, and nowadays the noisy racket of Stampede Solary's big power-driven concentrator thundered every day. Familiar landmarks of the town were lost in an ugly jumble of new buildings, and there was a constant influx of men whose presence would never have been tolerated in Rainbow a year ago. It was the old story of law and order in retreat before the mushroom boom of gold.

Across the street, Marshal Alec Bourne — Old Alec — spoke to his son. "What's that sin-sotted pack been up to now?" The marshal had grown old in his job and embittered during the past year. To see his quiet town turned into a roaring hell camp by outsiders had hit him hard.

"Another killing, far's I can make out," answered young Alec Bourne. He gave a savage yank to his hat brim. "Make me your deputy, dad, and let me go after Solary! He's robbed us, taken over the town and smashed every law, and laughs at us for trying to stop him!"

Old Alec turned a sour face to his son. "I wish," he stated, "you'd get that off your mind! I've told you, time an' again, it'd mean buckin' that whole crowd. How in thunder could *you* do it? Think you're a better man than me?"

Young Alec said no more, but it seemed to him that his father could be the most mule-headed man he knew. Sometimes he suspected that it was a matter of stubborn pride, a refusal on the part of Old Alec to admit himself an impotent and frustrated failure.

The Brindle Kid got to the point of his story. "Brothers, we all three had a grudge against that big hell buster! Me an' Blackfoot, we got the rough side of him once, down in San Rafe two years ago. An' he'd pulled some works on Stamp, one in time in Tombstone. Right, Stamp?"

Stampede Solary nodded. He stood by the doors of the Concordia, which he owned — a pale man with a bony forehead and keen, narrow, intelligent face. He was secretly amused at the Kid, but he carefully kept any look of contempt out of his eyes. "That's right, Kid," he murmured. "We scorched the devil himself, this trip."

Blackfoot Roen, silent and morose, merely looked on with leaden, half-shut eyes. It was known that he had once been caught and scalped by Blackfoot Indians while stealing their horses, but had recovered and escaped to live with a perpetual headache. He was never seen without a hat or with a smile.

"He was ridin' along a canyon rim," explained the Kid to the crowd. "Lookin' for a way down out o' the storm, I reckon. Didn't even see us. We sure showed him a quick way down!" He laughed aloud like a boy at a joke. "When I got off my shot, he just fell out o' his saddle an' down the canyon, slam through the brush! There wasn't no way to climb down after him along there, an' the storm was fierce, so we caught his horse an' came on home. Soon's this ol' windy season's past, I'm goin' on a hunt for his carcass. He's got heavy bounty on him these days, an' with a ring-tailed catawampus like him you're doin' mighty good to get him any ol' way, front or back!"

He teetered on his high heels, proud as a painted brave with a parfleche full of new scalps. "If we didn't finish him, he can't get far, nohow. That ol' Harina Desert, she's a death trap for any man afoot!"

Westward in the far distance from the tree-belted Mogollons, the high ranges ceased and the land swept downward to the blasting, mirage-haunted Harina Desert. Mexicans had it figured out that the unholy basin had been given to Satan to play with, in an attempt to keep him out of mischief. In line with his taste for a particular kind of awful beauty, Old Nick had filled it full of sand, heat, black saw-toothed ridges, and jagged red pinnacles. But after he'd had his fun, he used it for his private reservoir of somber destruction, drawing from it whenever he ran short of material elsewhere. The blinding seasonal sand storms marked the yearly visit of *El Diablo* spooning out fresh supplies from the inexhaustible reserves of the Harina.

In between the sand storms there was silence so dead and complete that it ached the ear. And then it was that the endless mirage took on voice as well as vision, luring the lost traveler to gibbering insanity in his vain quest of the unseen multitude calling him to cool cloisters of green trees and shady streams.

The man who dragged himself slowly up the long basalt ridge was hearing those voices, but his tenacious mind rejected them, refusing to trade harsh reality for beguiling fancies.

"Blood ringing in my ears."

Although it hurt his parched throat and cracked his lips to talk, he muttered it as a spoken fact which he could remember and cling to later as things got worse with him. He was in a desperately bad way, but he would retain sanity to the end. The night had been long and intolerable. He had tramped steadily through the cool darkness, making as much time as he could, merciless to bruised muscles that cried out for rest and ease, refusing to admit himself beaten by disaster. Morning had found him staggering to the foot of this ridge. The day would be worse, much worse, with the crushing heat, lack of water, and fast dehydrating of his battered, pain-racked body.

The sun rose slowly, dissipating the masses of riotous color that earlier gathered in the low eastern sky, and the sky turned to a hard, brazen blue. The somber red pinnacles took on a glow as the sun touched them, and black rimrock grew sharper edged against the tawny yellow of the sand. The night's coolness lingered, soon to be sucked away and replaced by the sun's imperturbable heat. The man raised his head as he crawled with bleeding hands up the ridge, hopeful for shelter from the sun. Perhaps on the other side of this basalt barrier there might be something, if only a hole that he could crawl into during the day. He looked back over the desert, and saw no shimmering mirages to match the whispering voices in his ears. They would come later. By noon this sun-parched hell would be falsely alive with them.

"Too early for the heat waves as yet."

He muttered that, too, aloud, as a tangible explanation of the phenomenon to come. The mirages would not fool him, any more than did the whispering voices. They were as much a part of this wilderness as the wild, forlorn beauty of it, and they belonged to its perils. A man had to include them in his estimate of chances, when setting about crossing the Harina. He would have been out of the desert by now, if bad luck had not conspired with both man and nature to topple him into catastrophe.

To think of the recent past, calmly and objectively, helped keep his clear senses from dwelling too deeply upon his hurts. For weeks he had been on the dodge, living almost constantly in the saddle, a lone wolf hunted and hard pressed for the price that he carried on his head. And it stemmed from the political aspirations of a man he had never seen — a territorial governor who, seeking high Federal office, was anxious to wind up his term with a record. To lay by the heels this man, who now crawled wearily and doggedly up a basalt ridge in the desert, would go far toward building up that desired record.

This man was notorious, a tall figure with a stormy reputation that ran close to legend. He was the peg upon which was hung a thousand deeds for which no other culprit could be found. For years he had gone his tumultuous way, smoking out all traps set for him, until lawmen had given up and tacitly called a truce. But now, under the ambitious and implacable hand of the governor, the combined resources of the whole territory were turned loose against him.

Bounty hunters were trailing him in bands, dazzled by the price offered for him. Sheriffs and town marshals, once apt to walk the other way when he appeared, were now buckling on extra guns and scanning every stranger. Hard penalties had been declared in force against anybody who might aid him. He had become the most famous fugitive in the territory, and the most widely sought, riding roughshod through the law whenever it got in his way, and having scores of enemies on both sides of it, he had always taken what he needed from any source and paid for it in one fashion or another.

But it had remained for some unknown bushwhackers to rip the bottom out of his sack. With his tall head bowed against the storm's wind and cutting sand, he had not even glimpsed them. They must have been behind some rocks, sheltering themselves from the storm, and recognized him as he rode by. He had no recollection of tumbling down into the canyon, and the sky had darkened when he came to his senses near the bottom. With blood-blinded eyes and a torn and battered body, climbing out had been a job.

He thought, with a shred of dour humor: "Hell, I don't even know who to cuss for it!"

He struggled the rest of the way up to the ragged crest of the ridge, and looked upon a monotony of more sand and black areas of broken malpais. A range of low hills, not far to the north, had the appearance of dry heaps of pepper and salt. The desert wind of the morning had died away. Nothing moved. The land was empty.

He sat down stiffly, his unsurrendering mind still an instrument of deliberate precision that kept searching for possibilities. At last he quit straining his bloodshot eyes. With a touch of grim fatalism, he took a broken cigar from the breast pocket of his black broadcloth coat, and clamped strong white teeth on the end of it.

"Well," he muttered hoarsely, "it begins to look like we've run all out of chips, hanged if it don't!"

The Rev. Elmore Topcliff settled his small spare frame on the driver's seat of his huge old overland wagon, beside his daughter, Faith. After a last look around the night's camp site to make sure that he was forgetting nothing, he gathered up the lines and clucked to the six-mule team. Getting the customary lack of response from the mules, he appealed to their better judgment. He addressed them by names with which he had endowed them when he bought them two months before. The seller had assured him that they were as tractable as Mormon children, but upon inquiry had admitted that he himself was a Baptist.

"Now, Sihon, remember what happened to thy namesake for his willfulness! And you, Og — giant that you are — pull! Amorite, Anakim, wake up the Moabite there —"

The mules were not impressed. They were Spanish mules wiry, wayward, disdainful of reasoning, persuasion and the Old Testament.

Faith Topcliff laughed softly. She was very young, and she had her father's quiet and whimsical humor. "I'm afraid you'll never teach them a proper respect for you, dad, unless you learn to . . . ahem . . . talk to them in freighter's language."

"My education fails me there," the reverend admitted mildly, and picked up the whip. "My friends," he apologized, "you leave me no alternative but this." He swung the whip.

This the mules could appreciate. Their broad leather housings snapped taut, the heavy trace chains jingled, and the big canvas-topped wagon creaked cumbrously into motion. Another day's journey had begun, one of many.

They were children of Providence, both of them, the elderly man and the young girl. Trust was their armor against all disillusionment, and happy serenity their shield against fear. The girl gazed about her, interested in the scenery, liking it for its strangeness, seeing nothing of its lurking claws. Under her sunbonnet her face was a warm cameo, and the poetic Mexicans would have said that the sun had got into her eyes. The

Rev. Topcliff, wise in his gentle way, sometimes wondered what manner of man it would be who would bring even heightened aliveness and warmth to his daughter. He hoped for the best, as always.

The wagon trundled slowly away from the camp site, and rounded a long series of sheltering hills before straightening out for the southeast course. Faith gazed back at the hills as they were left behind.

"They look," she said musingly, "like heaps of pepper and salt, don't they?"

Almost an hour later she touched her father's arm. The wagon was dragging through the sandy lowland between the hills and a long basalt ridge, with the sun getting higher and hotter. "Dad, I do believe there's something moving over there! Near the foot of that ridge. See? Some kind of animal, and it acts as if it's injured. Why, look, it's rising up on — Dad, it's a man!"

The Rev. Topcliff changed course toward it, but another half-hour had elapsed before he halted the team within fifty yards of the lone man, and climbed down from the seat. For once in his life, as he came up to the man, he experienced a thrill of something close to superstitious awe. Beside her father, Faith stood rooted, her eyes very big.

CHAPTER
TWO

The lone man stood like a tall specter of carnage, blood-spattered, yet with a chilling air of remoteness and grave austerity. The same contradiction was in his garb. From his long black coat and wide, flat-crowned hat, to his plain black riding boots, he could have been thought a minister. But the reverend sensed at once that this was no brother of the cloth, unless it was some mortal species of black angel descended from grace to gun smoke. The ministerial coat was ripped, allowing a glimpse of two crossed gun belts heavily studded with shells.

But it was the face that convinced the reverend. Blood, scratches, dirt, and an ugly wound near the black hair line, could not hide the fundamental qualities of that face. It was dark, stamped with ruthlessness and a hawklike strength. The nose was bold, predatory, the forehead broad, and the wide mouth was touched with a ghost of sardonic humor. The deep-set eyes, gray and bleak as winter sleet, held a terrible calmness that belonged nowhere between the two extremes of saint or sinner. The thought of Satan came to the mind of the reverend.

Satan inclined his tall, bloodied head. He said in a harsh voice that was strangely flattened: "Thanks for turnin' off your course."

The reverend grew aware of some kind of immense force in the man. Although the somber-garbed giant merely stood there, it was as if he were concentrating an inner power and waging a silent battle. It dawned upon the reverend that the man was hanging onto consciousness by the sheer will to do so.

"I . . . we . . . you must let us help you," he stammered, and an odd sense of formality caused him to introduce himself. "My name is Topcliff . . . er . . . *Rev.* Topcliff."

Saturnine humor came out fleetingly on the hard, wide mouth. "Glad to know you. My name's Devlin. *Preacher* Devlin!"

The grip slipped, and the strong will relinquished its losing fight. Like a very tired man, Preacher Devlin — top-flight gambler, master gun fighter, and fugitive at large — pitched over in his first step toward the wagon. He was quite unconscious while the reverend and Faith dragged him into the wagon and the reverend, as he unpacked his medical kit, sternly reminded himself that the Good Samaritan had not allowed adverse appearance to deter him from giving succor.

Later, with the wagon in motion, Preacher Devlin suddenly opened glittering eyes and began to talk in a deep growl of things that the reverend only dimly comprehended. They were only scraps of talk, let loose by a cool and dominant mind that had temporarily slipped control, but they conjured up some sinister visions. The Rev. Topcliff looked into that strong, satanic face, and he shivered a little. Saving brands from the burning was his life work, but this wounded man of mystery was something much more than a burning brand. This was one of the pagan masters who stoked and ruled sin's dark fire.

Out of the cloudy pit, Preacher Devlin fought upward to a lucid moment. He said distinctly: "I ought to warn you. It's dangerous to help me. You may regret it."

The reverend had much the same thought, although he knew nothing of the circumstances. But he shook his head. "A Christian act is never regretted by a Christian," he said simply.

The chill gray eyes regarded him. No sort of emotion softened their hardness, but some of the cynicism left the grim mouth. "If ever you're in need of help, yourself, bear me in mind. Call on me for anything, any time. Remember that. This is a debt. I pay my debts."

Then clarity passed and gave way to more mutterings, and the reverend turned to his daughter, who was driving. "Faith," he asked, "please pay less attention to . . . er . . . the talk in here!"

Obediently, the girl faced front again, flushing, but she was privately sure that her father failed to understand the fundamental significance of those alien, forceful phrases of Preacher Devlin. She had never before met unsubdued power, nor an untamed man. Now, meeting them, she ascribed to them nobility and strong virtues. This was the way, she thought hazily,

101

that the mighty Thor might have talked in his sleep after flinging his thunderbolts at the malignant horde, or Joshua after crashing down the walls of Jericho. A heightened aliveness and warmth ran through her, and she drove on with almost a sense of glory.

After a while, when the deep muttering had ceased, the reverend took his place on the driver's seat. "We must travel slowly and make early camp, for his sake," he murmured, and brightened as a thought occurred to him. "I think I shall use this incident as the basis of my first sermon in Rainbow!"

Like a heavily loaded barge under sail, the canvas-topped wagon rocked slowly along the high rim of Contention Creek, approaching the town of Rainbow. It drew some interest, most of it aimed at the girl sitting beside the gray little man on the driver's seat.

The workers scattered along the creek bed were of the usual run of fortune seekers, with a generous leavening of the tough and lawless. But where a big concentrating machine shook and rattled under the power of a steam engine, the men around it conformed to a more definite type. No misfits and wandering failures, these; their like was a standard quality to be found among gun-slingers of the top rank wherever the pay was highest. But to the Rev. Topcliff they were all men, future members of his flock, and he gazed almost paternally upon them as he drove his wagon along the rim trail.

The reverend and Faith had never before seen placer workings. They looked down at sluice boxes and rockers, and the big concentrator intrigued them with its elaborate setup. It stood on a wide bench of the upper bank, a mammoth with a sloping deck, many riffles, and a feed hopper. They saw an iron vessel like an oversized tub, with a cable and dragline running from it high above the creek to a rocky promontory on the far side. Atop the promontory was a huge kettle and firebox, and more armed men stood around up there.

"The ingenuity of man is quite amazing," murmured the reverend.

"'Specially where gold's concerned!" came the dry comment from within the wagon, and the two on the driver's seat turned.

With a bandaged hand raising the edge of the wagon canvas, Devlin lay peering out. "Is this Rainbow we're enterin'?" he queried.

The reverend nodded brightly. "Yes, this is my destination at last. Well find a doctor here for you, I'm sure."

Devlin lowered the canvas. "We won't bother. You're good-enough doctor for me." He studied his hands, badly gashed by climbing, bandaged by the reverend. The bullet score in his head sometimes made his eyes throb, and his muscles were stiff. He was in bad shape to meet big trouble. "I'd just as soon stay under cover for a spell, reverend."

Seeing the reverend's look of worry, he said more gently: "Most men have their enemies. It happens I've got a lot. If it were known where I am an' the shape I'm in, they'd be headin' my way in packs! I'll quit your wagon as soon as I can, but not by daylight!"

"I'm sorry," the reverend said troubledly. "I was thinking of mentioning you in my first sermon here."

Devlin eyed him, liking him, but grimly meditating that between himself and death stood only this mild little pilgrim. He quoted gravely: "'Tell it not in Gath . . . publish it not in the street of Askelon!'"

Driving on into Rainbow, the reverend whispered to Faith: "He actually quoted from the Old Testament!"

"Of course," said Faith serenely. "Why shouldn't he?"

As the wagon lurched into the deep ruts of Rainbow's main street, it had to come to a halt because of a shouting crowd that jammed the street. Somebody was attempting to ride a magnificent, long-limbed black horse, and raising considerable dust about it.

The black horse didn't care for his rider, nor for the noisy crowd of onlookers, and he proceeded to make known his disapproval. He took two jumps, high and wide, and the stirrup leathers popped like pistol shots. But that was just a feeler. He threw in a high roller and came down all stiff-legged, jarring his rider's bones from ankle to skull. That was for punishment. Then he got down to real business.

He pulled a pretty series of weaving bucks, tightened them up into a rapid display of sunfishing acrobatics that made him look like a black streak of animated rubber, and wound it up by swapping ends faster than a cat changing its mind. That did the trick. Next thing, the Brindle Kid was sitting in the street with his hands full of dirt and his nose running blood. The crowd howled, and somebody caught the black and led him off to the Concordia livery stable.

Devlin, peering out between the front canvas flaps of the wagon, breathed words that did not belong to the testaments. The glitter lurked again in the sleety depths of his eyes, but not from any incipient delirium. There were faces in the crowd that he recognized from other days, chief among them those of the Brindle Kid, Blackfoot Roen, and Stampede Solary. The big black horse he had known at once; it was his own, an animal second only to himself in notoriety. Solary, he noticed, was studying the reverend's daughter with quick interest.

He began tearing the bandages from his injured hands, and while he worked at them, he watched a rangy young fellow come up to the halted wagon. The young fellow had a straight good-humored look about him, and for that reason alone he stood out from the crowd. His candid young eyes were mostly on Faith, but he spoke respectfully to the Rev. Topcliff.

"Can I help you get located, sir?" he offered. "My name's Alec Bourne."

The reverend's trustful smile came forth. "Why, thank you. I'm the Rev. Elmore Topcliff, and this is my daughter, Faith. I was asked to come here to your town last year, but at that time — dear me, why is that young man shouting at us?"

The Brindle Kid, having failed to impress the audience with his riding, was off on another tack, and in a vicious mood that he hid with clownery. With his sleek head to one side, he stood braying in the street and pointing at the wagon mules. He capered to a crowded hitching rack, got himself a red Navaho saddle blanket, and came on the prance like a toreador, waving it. The Spanish mules shivered expectantly and cocked their long ears at him, perfectly willing to cooperate in a plunging stampede through the town.

Young Alec Bourne stood by the front end of the wagon. With tight mouth and a hand to his holster, he started around the team to bar the advance of the Brindle Kid, but two close-spaced shots, followed soon after by a third, caused him to yank out his gun and halt. The reverend ducked, and so did Faith, their ears ringing from the reports just above and behind their heads. They were the only ones who could have told with any accuracy where the shots came from. The peak-crowned sombrero flew from the head of the Brindle Kid, and as he dropped the saddle blanket and cut his left hand hipward, the second bullet slapped that hand. The third shot, fired as if on after-thought following a brief pause, took care of his right-hand gun; its poking bone handle burst apart from the impact of the bullet that struck and wrecked the breech. After the first startled moment, the crowded street hushed, all eyes on the young killer standing hatless and amazed by the crumpled saddle blanket.

The Brindle Kid didn't look so perky now, but more like a soulless young gnome that had got a thrashing. He stared down at his dripping left hand, and then at Alec Bourne and the drawn gun. A shudder shook his body, and the raging wildness that leaped into his eyes was equal to insanity. His warped and perverted pride, the sustenance of his lurid life, had twice been pierced within five minutes.

"You . . . you —" Profanity of the gutter, mucky and grotesque, poured from his thinned, twisted lips. At a nod from Solary, morose Blackfoot Roen stepped over to the Kid and led him away, still cursing.

Marshal Bourne came plodding along, frowning at everybody, a soured old man trying to cling to the last empty vestige of his waned authority. As he came up to the wagon, Old Alec saw the gun in his son's hand, and he made the same error that the Brindle Kid and the crowd had made. Anger darkly flushed his lined face.

"Tryin' to be a gun fighter, huh?" he barked. "You young fool —"

"Really, you are quite mistaken, marshal," interrupted the reverend. "That young man —"

He was interrupted, himself, at that point, by Devlin's hand through the canvas, prodding him silent. And just then four worried-looking individuals came following in the wake of Rainbow's angry marshal. Old Alec Bourne raised his face to the little man on the wagon seat. "What did you start to say? Who're you, anyway?"

Young Alec gave the answer. "He's the Rev. Topcliff, dad. Remember that name?"

"Jumpin' Jehosaphat!" groaned one of the four men, and threw up his hands in dismay. "As if we ain't got trouble enough, without that! What did you come for, reverend? There ain't no place here for you — not now. Holy cow, not now!"

CHAPTER
THREE

The man who was doing all the lamenting had eyes that were magnified large behind thick spectacles, and a nervous manner. "I'm Bob Peattie, the mayor," he made himself known, "and these three gents are the town council — Colonel Rorick, Harvey Colville, and Bat Brown. Why, reverend, it's over a year since we wrote and asked you here, and you wrote back and refused."

"A year ago your town did not need me," the reverend pointed out. "It obviously does now, so I came. Have you a church?"

"We-ell, we did have last year." Mayor Peattie looked around at the councilmen, but they only gazed down at their boots. "But not now," he amended, and blinked at a dance hall along the street. "It's been . . . uh . . . turned into something else."

The understanding reverend sighed. "Never mind; I can use a tent for the time being. But I *would* appreciate some kind of living quarters for myself and my daughter."

The mayor and council, by mute but unanimous vote, turned that matter over to Marshal Bourne, and retired, mumbling good wishes on the reverend. For a minister of the gospel to come to a roaring hell camp like Rainbow created a very delicate problem, and they wanted none of it, so they loaded it onto the sagging shoulders of the harassed old lawman. Old Alec scowled helplessly after them. His baffled expression said that he expected worst and didn't know what to do about it. Squinting out through the slit of the wagon canvas, Devlin saw no happy solution in sight as yet, either.

"Livin' quarters, huh? I dunno, I swear." Old Alec wandered around the wagon, inspecting it absently, stalling for time. The town was packed. Cubbyholes were renting for five dollars a night. "Mebbe I could . . . I dunno. How much stuff you got with you?"

He poked his head between the rear flaps for a look inside. After a queer gulp, he said no more, nor did he move. Young Alec, curious about that behavior, joined him. He, too, looked inside. And he, too, froze silent.

With a long-barreled gun tilted in his scarred right hand, Devlin said softly: "One yelp, hombres, an' it'll be your last, I promise you!"

He knew by their faces that they had recognized him at once, and knew that he had handed them the shock of their lives. His appearance and description were too well known, too well published for him to escape immediate detection in any crowd, anywhere. They might have entertained a natural faint doubt that he was dead, in spite of seeing his horse brought in, and the Brindle Kid's bragging. Preacher Devlin had been known to emerge from other disasters just as seemingly final. But they certainly hadn't looked for him to turn up alive in Rainbow, and in a minister's wagon of all places.

Old Alec swallowed several times. "It's the law you got your gun on, Preacher!" he brought out at last, and then appeared to realize that it was a futile and unnecessary statement. His badge was large and in sight, and Devlin had never been reputed to show any particular discrimination between lawmen and lesser mortals.

"So here's where those shots came from!" young Alec said. "I was wondering. Shucks, dad, you know I don't shoot that good!" He stared into the forbidding face of the notorious gun fighter, and added: "But I can try if I have to!"

The reverend and Faith looked in through the front. "Oh, dear me!" murmured the reverend. He was aghast at what he saw.

Not so, Faith. "How dare you pry into our wagon!" she challenged the two Bournes.

Old Alec blinked at her. "Now you looka here, young lady! You an' your pa are hidin' a . . . a mighty bad hombre in your wagon! Yessir, a mighty bad —"

"You don't know what you're talking about!" she flashed back at him hotly. "Do you call it bad to stop a gunman from frightening a team? Why didn't *you* stop that man? Isn't that what you're paid to do?" Her eyes blazed at young Alec. "All *you* did was take the credit for shooting at him!" she ended scornfully.

Her young face glowed with righteous indignation. She wasn't the quiet, demure little parson's daughter now. She was all wound up. Old Alec struggled for

110

speech, and only sputtered. Young Alec went as red as a shamed criminal at the bar. The reverend gazed at his daughter in alarm, not knowing what to make of all this.

To Devlin it was something of a novel experience, having a young slip of a girl like this one taking up for him so wholeheartedly. He regarded Old Alec with some dry humor.

"You're pretty near outnumbered, marshal," he observed, and motioned with his gun. "Climb up in here, you two, an' guide the reverend to his new quarters. An' don't get any foolish ideas, on the way. If things pop, you're apt to be first on the list to go!"

Old Alec glared at him. "For one thing," he stated chokedly, "there ain't an empty room in this town to be had for —"

"In that case," cut in Devlin, "well just have to take you up on your invitation, an' move in with you! Drive on, reverend!"

The marshal stamped up and down his own living-room floor like a scandalized bear crowded out of its den, darting glowering looks at the long, black-coated figure of Devlin, who had taken possession of the couch. Quarters had been made in the marshal's house for the Topcliffs. Young Alec, rising creditably to the occasion, had waved away their doubts and protests. Plenty of room, he said. He and his father, he assured them, were only too glad to share their house with refined folks. Somewhat pointedly, he neglected to include the Preacher in that last statement.

111

Rev. Topcliff, with a shine in his mild eyes, spoke of his work. He had already located a site for his tabernacle tent, on a level space of waste land not fifty yards from the rear of the house. Tomorrow he would begin building benches and a pulpit. Sunday, he would hold his first service. In a few weeks, he predicted, the town would build a real church.

"Don't bet on that," remarked Devlin. "This is a wolf town, an' it'd take more than a Bible to tame it!"

" 'They shall give tithes and cause a church to be built,' " quoted the reverend, a stem edge to his voice.

Devlin shrugged his broad shoulders. "An' I'll sit in the congregation!"

The reverend gave him a long, pensive look. "That alone would make all my work worthwhile," he declared gravely, and walked out.

As soon as the door closed, Old Alec stopped his pacing and swung a gnarled finger at Devlin. "You can't hold me a prisoner in my own house, blast it!" he declared.

Devlin gazed musingly at the irate old lawman, and eased himself to another position on the couch. "No," he agreed. "I can't watch you day an' night, that's sure." He thought of all the hunters scouring the country for him. When the report got spread around that he was dead, bushwhacked by Stampede Solary and a couple of hirelings, there would be a letup in the hunting. Then he would be able to make a dash for Old Mexico, and be clear out of this country before the next hue and cry stormed loose.

It wasn't going to be easy to lie in hiding, right here in Rainbow, but the desperate situation demanded it, and so did Devlin's battered body. Just a few days would do it. But if the slightest hint or whisper got out that he was here, he'd be blown up for keeps. Even if he could hold off the Solary crowd, there'd be the governor's men and the free-lance bounty hunters riding fast this way in droves to ring him in. Well, the reverend wouldn't let it out, and neither would Faith. They weren't as yet aware of the circumstances, but he'd asked them to keep quiet about him, and they could be trusted. Young Alec Bourne wouldn't talk, either. He was pretty obviously in love with the girl, and didn't want to bring any trouble upon her and her father. This old law hound here, though, was a different proposition.

"I wonder now," Devlin muttered, "if I dare put you on your word — or if you'd give it!"

Bourne narrowed his eyes. He was wise enough to recognize the advantage that still remained to him. "Devlin," he said evenly, "you're on one almighty big powder keg — the worst ever! An' you ain't in no shape right now to handle it if it goes off! That Solary crowd is a mighty tough combination, let me tell you, an' that's leavin' out all the others around the country who'd give their teeth to get you. But I know about you. I know what's in your mind. You're figgerin' to lay low till you're ready, then bust out o' here an' blow this town apart before you hit for the border! Well, this is still my town, bad as 'tis, an' I'll be hanged if —" He paused.

Devlin was slowly shaking his head. "You're on the wrong bronc," he contradicted harshly. "I'll kick over no kegs in this town, now or later. But not on your account."

With the wind taken out of his sails, the marshal tugged at his mustache. "I guess," he said finally, "the rev'rend saved your life, out there in the Harina. Is it because he'd catch holy Ned for it if it got known you're here an' he brung you? That it? By jacks, Devlin, mebbe you're almost human, after all!"

"I figure," Devlin grunted, "he's liable to spill more genuine hell over this cussed town than I could, that's all! He's a pretty good little hombre. Asks no questions. Hanged if I don't like him."

"So do I. He'll do to take along, all right."

"Yeah. He's going to need plenty help here. I'd do it, but that wouldn't work out. It's your job. Don't let him down, *sabe*?"

"Sure," agreed the marshal. He grined faintly and frostily. "Mebbe you an' me ain't so far apart in some, ways, at that. When'll you be leavin'?"

"About Sunday night, I reckon, if the town's quiet enough. I'll raise no ruckus leaving, if I can help it."

"Your word on that?"

"Uh-huh."

"Well, I reckon I can give my word, too. I'm a clam till Sunday night. No need to watch me."

Old law dog and veteran long rider exchanged brief nods, all that either of them needed to make the deal binding. They understood each other, from opposite sides of the law's high fence.

114

In a town like Rainbow Sunday night could be expected to be a resounding echo of Saturday night — rip-roaring and wild. But this Sunday night was different. No revivalist could have wished for a better crowd than the Rev. Topcliff was drawing into his big canvas tabernacle. Most of the saloons and dance halls were quiet, and even the Concordia had closed its doors. For half an hour there had been a steady flow toward the tent behind the marshal's house.

It was such a well-behaved crowd that Devlin was inclined to distrust it on principle. Ministers and revivalists did saloon owners no good, and the owners could be expected to fight against reform. But the saloonmen and gamblers of Rainbow seemed to be cooperating tonight to make the reverend's opening skirmish against the devil a solid success. It looked too good to be true.

However, from a rear window of the marshal's darkened house, Devlin watched the last of the crowd troop into the lighted tent, and he saw nothing to verify his suspicions. Nobody was carrying any dead cats, or paper "snakes" of gunpowder, or solemnly leading a beer-hiccuping burro into the meeting. The confused shadows on the tent canvas settled to an orderly pattern, voices ceased murmuring, and there came the time of silence. Then, faint but clear in the hushed night, sounded the gentle, pleased voice of the reverend:

"Dear people . . . friends . . . I cannot express in words my gladness at seeing so many of you here tonight. I . . . I am really overwhelmed —"

Devlin turned away from the opened window, and the hesitant voice faded from his hearing as he made his way through the house toward the front door. Now was as good an hour as any in which to slip quietly out of Rainbow. There was only one detail to attend to, and that was the stealing of his own horse from the Concordia stable. He hoped to do that undetected. Outside of that, he would forgo taking a crack at those who had done him dirt in the Harina, for the sake of the little reverend, who had helped him out of it. Also, it would give him more time to reach Mexico before folks became aware that he was still alive and on his way.

He opened the front door, and the voice of the reverend reached to him again in the hush: "— so let us turn to the one hundred and thirty-third Psalm: 'Behold, how good a thing it is, in unity to dwell — '"

Then the lid blew off.

First, giving the cue and blasting the solemn quiet, rose the braying whoop of the Brindle Kid. It rang out through the town, and its tail was lost in the discordant uproar that it touched off. Yells, catcalls, roaring laughter — the splintering crash of a flimsy bench being smashed over another — a bottle that hit and shivered the canvas, and a thunder of exploding guns. The Concordia crowd was hoo-rawing the little reverend without mercy and without the saving grace of good humor. They were out to wreck his tent and humble fixings, and run him out of town.

Devlin stood very still in the open door, his hard mouth drawn down, eyes pale and oblique. As the racket got louder, he gave his head a short and savage shake. This was none of his affair. He had nothing to bet on a penniless little pilgrim who was simple enough to think that he could uplift a hell hole like Rainbow. His affair was to quit town like a shadow and head south, and on doing this his life depended. Better to get his horse and go, taking advantage of the racket, and leave the problem in the marshal's lap. It was the marshal's job, anyway, and he'd talked as though he was prepared to handle it — he and that husky son of his.

But still Devlin didn't leave, and now he was fighting himself, fighting down his impulses and calling himself a fool for having them. He tugged down the wide brim of his black, flat-crowned hat. "Damn it, I've got to get out o' here!" he muttered, and stepped out onto the street.

Yonder was the Concordia stable, unwatched and unguarded, his big black inside, ready for him to saddle and ride away. To the south lay Mexico. He could be well on his way, come morning, and then all hell couldn't catch up with him, for he'd have under him the best horse in the territory and an open track ahead. Maybe it wasn't as bad as it sounded from here, in that tent. Maybe it was just a bunch of roughnecks having fun, and after the marshal had them corralled in the *juzgado* they'd pay their fines and shake hands with the reverend. New sky pilgrims had that kind of rough initiation to contend with, often enough, and if they were good sports they became popular fixtures in the town.

Somebody came pattering around the house and ran full into Devlin. It was Faith, sobbing, terror in her eyes, and that terror wiped away all notions about rough fun. She clung to the tall, somber gun fighter, and in this instant it came to Devlin as a dim flash of ominous warning, that the girl showed no slightest timidity with him. She appeared to regard him as a kind of champion, a reliable and invincible guardian to whom she could turn to in extremity.

"Help him! They've all gone mad!" Her small hands pulled at him. "Oh, please — quick — help him! They're —"

"What's the marshal doing?" Devlin broke in. "An' Alec?"

"A lot of men have got them in a corner, holding guns to them — laughing at them!"

"Where's your father?"

"In the pulpit. Just standing there . . . standing there and crying! They're all shouting at him and throwing things at him! Oh, please — hurry!"

Devlin's face was a baleful mask. He said in a mutter, talking mostly to himself: "If I get into this, my last chance is busted! If I throw away this chance, I'll never get another! They'll make sure o' that. That damned governor —"

"Oh, please!" The girl was hearing nothing of what he was saying. Her mind was still back in that tent. "You I promised! You promised dad if ever he needed help, you'd give it — that you owed him a debt and you'd pay it any time he asked!"

118

Devlin brought his bleak eyes back to the pleading young face, and gave a slight start. "That's right, I did. I remember that." He uttered a short laugh, and his eyes suddenly took on a glitter of violent recklessness that he was not I wholly reluctant to welcome. "All right, girl — let's go to church meetin'!"

CHAPTER
FOUR

The tent was a bedlam, the sides shaking and shadows jumbled on the canvas. Some of them in there were howling a saloon song now, in between shooting off their guns and breaking benches. Others apparently were thrusting at the tent poles, making the lighted lanterns swing and dance dangerously.

Devlin got to one end of the long tent, pulled up the edge of the canvas, and ducked through. His ministerial coat hung open, and his scarred hands were spread ready, but for the moment he was unnoticed in the riotous tumult. Directly before him he saw the pulpit, plain and unpainted, the best that Rev. Topcliff had been able to build from materials at hand and from a slender purse. Devlin was behind it, the reverend's back toward him. The reverend stood up there in his little pulpit, arms hanging, shaking his grayed head in a dazed, incredulous way, while chaos raged before him and jeering voices howled at him. The core of the wreckers was the Solary mob. Other men — the hangers-on, the riffraff of the town — were following the lead.

Catching the reverend by the back of his coat, Devlin lifted him out of the pulpit as if plucking a marooned kitten down from a tree. The reverend turned a white and quivering face to him, but no immediate recognition came into his shocked eyes. He had a look of horror about him, and that look pulled the last tight notch on the Preacher's anger.

Devlin stepped up into the pulpit, and his pair of heavy guns dented the wood as he slammed them down. His eyes, glimmering with cold wrath, ranged over the rioting mob. He saw Solary, the first to sight him, jerk and go motionless and wax-hued. Then his sardonic side came uppermost, bringing with it the saturnine humor that cloaked his most reckless, ruthless moods.

"Preacher Devlin — taking over the service!" he thundered, and the metallic edge of his voice knifed through the uproar. Each of his guns roared a single shot apiece. One man, wrenching at a center pole, jerked away a hand that was shy a finger. Another, swinging a wooden bench high over his head, ended his laughter and fell asprawl with the bench and a broken shoulder.

Like a powerful brake being clamped down on a team of bronco brutes stampeding downhill, the uproar faltered and died away. The crowd stood all askew and stilled, and abruptly there was only harsh breathing to rustle the new silence. Staring, unbelieving eyes were seeing a ghost in the pulpit — a tall, black ghost, satanic and armed, ready and willing to trade gun smoke — where before had stood a bowed, broken little minister.

Somebody muttered huskily, sounding loud in the lack of other noises: "It's a damn lie! It ain't him! Can't be — can't be —"

The Brindle Kid was known as well for his nerve as for his brag. His mouth changed shape to the contortioning movements of his tongue and lips, and at last he said in little more than a whisper: "How, Preacher!" He had one hand in a sling, and he wore only one gun now, but he was crazy enough to take a chance if he thought he saw one.

"'Lo, Kid. Sit down." Devlin's ominous stare bored at the young killer, and the Brindle Kid slowly sat down. "All o' you sit down! *Sit down, I say!*"

Again a long-barreled gun blared from the pulpit. In the rear of the tent, a man dropped something and swayed out through the exit, his face sick and all his rashness drained out. Devlin did not watch him go. His baleful, mocking stare kept sweeping over the mob, and he held his guns tilted, the hammers thumbed back.

He had them. The shocking amazement of seeing him appear in the pulpit like a specter from the dead had for the time petrified them, and they were all under his eyes. When they slowly began uprighting the benches and sitting on them, watching his poised guns, obeying him, Devlin knew that the high crisis was staved off for this moment at least. Having failed to call his hand right away, they could be dominated further before they blew up. Solary was the kingpin of this crowd, but he had brains and patience, and would not be likely to set off the explosion while sitting on the lid.

122

The Brindle Kid had chosen discretion, temporarily. Blackfoot Roen was dangerous, but he lacked initiative.

It was like holding the whip in a cage full of wild cats, each beast respectful of the whip, but the whole pack capable of swiftly seizing the mastery if it got any chance at all to organize. Devlin didn't figure to let that chance out of the bag.

From a rear corner of the tent, Marshal Bourne and Alec came forward together, carefully passing along the aisle of wooden benches. Both had been held there, raging and impotent under a dozen guns during the riot. Faith appeared, coming from one side of the tent and gazing at Devlin as if he were more than mere man. Alec paused by her and murmured something, but she only shook her head disregardingly, not even looking at him, and he bit his lip and passed by. The marshal glowered with a queer mingling of emotions at the Preacher.

Devlin banged a gun barrel on the pulpit. "It's pretty clear that this congregation's got no use for psalms," he drawled. "Maybe it'll suit better if we head right into the sermon — an' I want silence while I give it! *Sabe?* Reverend, what'll the subject be?"

He waited for a reply, while his compelling survey raked over the tensed faces before him. At last it came, low-voiced and solemn: "The story of Sodom and Gomorrah!"

Devlin nodded. Beneath the frozen calm of his irony, his mood was a white-hot flame, the flicker of it visible and sinister in his eyes. "Brethren!" he intoned, sonorous as a copper bell. "It once came to pass that a couple o' tough camps sprang up, like this Rainbow town, called Sodom an' Gomorrah. They finally got so ornery . . . Hm-m-m, just a minute. Hats off in church, heathens!"

He fired without apparent aim, and Solary's fine Stetson spun in the air with two new vents in it. Every other hat came off. It was the kind of casual, accurate shooting warranted to cause any dissenter to think long thoughts. The pulpit commanded a clear vantage over everybody in the tent, and the man-killing power of those two long guns needed no advertising.

Devlin went on, with the blandness of a lecturing judge. "This pair o' hell camps finally got so ornery tough, a posse of angels flew in one day an' cleaned 'em out. But a gent by the name of Lot, bein' a pretty square hombre, was tipped off that the big law was comin'. He gathered his folks an' took to the hills just in time. But his wife, with more idle curiosity than was good for her, looked back, although she'd been warned not to. That was her mistake. She got turned into a pillar o' salt. That's the sermon. Pass the collection plate, Faith!"

Obediently, Faith looked around for it, but it wasn't in sight.

"Use Solary's hat," Devlin told her. "Begin at the back row — an' let me know right away if any cheap noncomformer tries to hold out! Brethren, you're about to chip in for a new church, an' I want to see gold go into that hat. Nothin' less than twenty-dollar pieces! You've had your fun; now pay for it. As you drop in

124

your donations, walk out nice an' quiet, one at a time. Remember Lot's wife. The moral is: *Don't look back!"*

Late that night, Old Alec Bourne turned from peering out through the drawn shades of his front window, and his querulous glance lighted on Devlin. The gun master stood by the table with the reverend and Faith, counting coins. Mayor Peattie and the three councilmen were there, looking very uncertain of themselves, while young Alec stood doing nothing much more than looking miserably at Faith.

"I might've known you wouldn't quit without pullin' some kind o' rusty on this town!" Old Alec rasped. "Well, you ain't gettin' away with that money, there, I tell you that!"

Devlin raised his eyes from the heap of gold coins on the table, as he finished counting. "All I did was give a sermon," he pointed out dryly. "You'll admit it was needed bad." He shoved the money over to the reverend. "Don't feel backward about usin' this. They owed it to you, an' they gave it. You got enough there to build a church no town need be ashamed of."

Old Alec still bushed his brows angrily, stubbornly. "Half the town's hot on the prod, now you've showed y'self! Every door, alley an' hole out there has got shadows that don't belong! It means a battle if you step outside!"

Devlin gave his crossed belts a hitch. "Quit fretting. I said I'd leave tonight, an' I will!" The turbulent urge of the gun fighter was alive in him, with its component quality of icy calm that blanked all expression from his eyes and made even harder the granite cast of his face.

"But you can't leave now!" spoke up the reverend.

"Why can't I?"

"You said," the reverend explained patiently, "that if this town caused a church to be built, you would join the congregation!" His kindly eyes held a determined gleam. "Well, here is the money to build that church. The town gave it. They are causing a church to be built!"

"Besides," chimed in Faith, "we still need your help! As long as this town remains as bad and lawless as it is, we'll always need you! You can't leave us; you gave your word!"

Devlin nearly winced. "Now, listen!" he growled. "You don't understand. I can't stay, now that I'm known to be here. I've got to be on my way, before —"

"But we do need you," insisted the reverend quietly. "We need you here, as much as you needed us in the desert!"

"I gave the marshal my promise that I'll pull out tonight. That's final!" Devlin felt somewhat grateful to Bourne for eliciting that promise from him, now. It was going to get him out of this, awkward situation. It meant sure death for him, if he stuck around here while the governor's army of hunters came pounding in from all directions. All he wanted was a smoky farewell to this town of Rainbow, and a fast ride south.

Mayor Peattie cleared his throat. "As far as that goes," he piped up, "the authorities of this town, as

126

represented by myself and the council, would not object to you staying here . . . ah . . . Mr. Devlin!"

"*Gracias!*" returned Devlin dryly. "Solary's got your town in his fist, an' the law's all shot to blazes, so you wouldn't object if I stayed — on your side! No bet, gentlemen! I've got myself to think of. Your town doesn't concern me."

"But it must, don't you see? Because it concerns us," put in Faith. "If you go, what will happen to us here?"

The town council went through their silent communion of exchanged glances. Colonel Rorick, a stiff-mannered man, spoke with genteel reserve. "Miss Topcliff is . . . hum . . . entirely justified in her fears. Solary holds the town, and he's a vengeful man. No scruples at all. He'd take it out on the reverend and . . . hum. Yes, indeed. Frankly, we can't vouch for the safety of anybody in Rainbow any more. Independent placer miners get murdered, and Solary's men take over their claims and workings. Solary even stole that big claim of his from the Bournes, and stole Alec's ideas on how to work it. We may as well admit that lawlessness has gone far past the point where our marshal can handle it. With all respect to you, Bourne — and to you, Alec — I think that was made evident tonight!"

"I believe," insinuated Mayor Peattie, "the marshal may now wish to say a few words. Eh, Bourne?"

Old Alec, looking older than he had a moment before, let his shoulders slump. "I s'pose you're right," he mumbled. "It's got way too big for me. If Devlin don't leave tonight, that's all right with me, I guess." He tramped out of the room, blinking heavily like a man who had lost something.

With his last excuse gone, Devlin felt trapped, like a wild hawk chained and ready for executioners. But a bullet and the desert had placed him under total obligation to the Topcliffs. His life belonged to them as long as they needed him, and he paid his bets and debts — always, and on both sides of the ledger.

"All right, reverend, you win! I'll stick as long as you need me."

"Thank you, my friend," replied the reverend, and in his eyes was a glow that Devlin darkly suspected boded him no good. It bespoke a rising hope of converting a certain law-smashing pagan to respectable ways and lawful pastures, in time.

Faith's young eyes were bright with a different kind of glow, as she gazed at Devlin. It was a look that made Alec tighten his mouth and grow lean in the face.

"Oh, I'm so glad!" she breathed, and Alec turned sharply away.

Devlin bit deeply into his chewed and unlighted cigar. He didn't mind so much the prospect of tangling some more with the Solary crowd. As for the governor's horde of hunters, well, they'd come when they'd come. He could face the event without any crumbling of his fatalism, and certainly without any panic. But he could very well do without the uplifting efforts of a sky pilgrim, the dazzled and mistaken worship of the pilgrim's innocent young daughter, and the red jealousy of a right-minded young fellow in love with that girl.

128

Such things were highly explosive and unpredictable in their potentialities.

He scowled the mayor and town councilmen out of the house, and those worthies departed unsure whether to congratulate themselves or not. Devlin knew their game. It suited them very well for him to stay and back up the reverend. His presence would draw the governor's law to Rainbow, and maybe they could induce all that law to clean up their town for them, when it got here. By means of his obligation and word to the Topcliffs, the mayor and council were using him as a foil against the Concordia crowd, and a sacrificial decoy to bring in big law.

Sometimes, Devlin meditated, respectable men evinced as much cunning strategy as the most wiry of outlaws.

CHAPTER
FIVE

Next day Devlin ran afoul of the reverend. He was striding out of the marshal's house, and found his path barred by the little churchman, who was just entering.

"You mustn't go out there, Devlin!" Topcliff said excitedly.

"Why not?"

"They're waiting for you! The town is like an armed camp!"

"That's why I'm going out!" Devlin's chill stare caused the reverend to flinch. "It's not my way to hide out from the like o' this!"

Faith appeared behind her father, and Alec with her. The marshal came plodding up, too. They gathered before the tall, grim-visaged gun fighter, and he sent his gaze beyond them at a half dozen men loitering in an alley across the street. The whole town was as hushed as a graveyard.

"It's got to come, I know that, Devlin," Old Alec said stonily. "We all know it. But you got to abide by the law while you're here!"

"D'you expect me to stay cooped up? I'll tame this town, or go to smash with it! When that's done, my bill's paid — an' I'll either be on my way, or you can bury me, reverend! It's got to be done today, an' the sooner the better!" Devlin had come to that decision during the night. Maybe he could pay his bill and still reach Old Mexico ahead of the hunting horde. He could feel that horde closing in on him, thundering in from all over the territory. The word must have gone out in the night, he knew, that the notorious fugitive had showed up in Rainbow, and the news would be spreading fast.

"Wait a few minutes, that's all I ask. Mayor Peattie's comin'." Old Alec passed a hand over his face. "He — I reckon he's comin' to ask you to take my badge. We had it out this mornin', him an' me, an' the council. They said I'm gettin' too old. This is my last day on the job."

Devlin kept his eyes on the alley. "I don't need any badge — yours or any other!"

Old Alec nodded. "I know. I know. But I'm still the marshal till Peattie gets here. After I step down, you can let 'er rip, 'cause I just won't give a hoot any more. Old an' worn-out, that's me. That's what they said. Old an' worn-out!" He came in, passed Devlin, and sat down. He fiddled absently with the badge on his vest, and stared at the floor. Marshal Alec Bourne, for thirty years the lawman of Rainbow, was all washed up.

Young Alec went and stood by his father, and the look he sent Devlin was bitter. The men, becoming conscious of being watched, vanished from the alley. Devlin came back in and stood by the front window, watching for the next pattern to shape up, ready to locate its possible flaws. The Concordia crowd spurred by enmity and the prospect of high bounty and knowing that peril stalked them as long as he lived, was out to get him if they could. Tonight, if he waited, might be too late; they'd have him ringed inside the house again, as they had last night, with sharpshooters posted to cut him down as soon as he emerged. Now was the time to step out and meet them at their game, in daylight, while they expected him to keep to cover.

A shot, a high yell, and a crashing of bottles suddenly came from inside the Concordia. It sounded as if some drunk had gone amuck in there. Another report cracked, and somebody uttered a pained cry. A dance-hall girl gave a raucous scream and quit abruptly at the pitch of it. Stampede Solary, himself, stepped hastily out through the Concordia doors and raised an urgent shout.

"Hey, where's the law? Fellow's gone crazy in here, shooting everybody! Where's that broken-down old plug of a marshal?"

Old Alec reared up out of his chair, bristling like an aged watch dog roused from reveries by a sound in the night. "Huh? What's he call me? Broken-down ol' plug! By jinks, I'll show 'em! Stand back, everybody; I'll tend to this! I'll show 'em what an ol' worn-out, broken-down plug like me can do, when he —" Old Alec's rumble trailed off as he barged out of the house and across the street to the saloon.

Young Alec took off after his father. The shooting started up again in the saloon before he got there. Then sudden silence, and seconds later a rapid pounding of hoofs beating away from the rear of the Concordia.

Somebody shouted loudly: "He got away all right, that hombre — but he sure scattered hell behind him!"

Mayor Peattie and the three councilmen came trotting into the Bourne house and hauled up against Devlin.

"What's happened?" blurted the mayor. "Has it started?"

"I reckon you could say it has," Devlin answered. "They've started to whittle us down, anyway! It might've been better for you hombres if I'd pulled out last night, or tried to. Because I stayed, it's brought things to a head this mornin' — an' you're all up to your necks in it with me!"

He gazed somberly through the window at the doors, of the Concordia. "There goes the last trace o' law this town had left! It was a plant, an' the old man walked slam into it. Maybe he didn't care. Maybe it's a pity you told him he was worn-out. It got under his hide. Solary called him worse, an' that did it. Pretty soon young Bourne'll be comin' back to tell us his dad's been shot. Yeah, here he comes now — carryin' him!"

Alec Bourne, with a new look of age and hardness on him, tramped in with his father in his arms and laid him carefully on the couch. Old Alec had his eyes open, and he said almost gently: "Don't take it so hard, young un. I lasted a long time. Too long, mebbe. Devlin —"

"What is it, marshal?"

"No need to call me that. I ain't the marshal here no more." Old Alec dragged a bloodied hand over his vest. His fingers curled around the badge and he tore it off. "She's all yours, an' welcome! Damn this town, anyway.

133

Give 'em law, Preacher — your kind o' law! Mine warn't strong enough. You an' the rev'rend . . . run the law an' the fear o' hell into 'em! Huh, rev'rend?"

"We'll try," said the reverend softly. "Won't we, Devlin?"

The Preacher took the badge. "Looks that way."

Old Alec grinned faintly. "Funny . . . the Preacher an' the rev'rend . . . teamed together! Good luck. Wish I could . . . hang around . . . an' watch —" His mouth went lax, and the reverend knelt.

Alec Bourne gazed down for a long time at the grayed, lined face, and at last he looked around him with slow, unseeing eyes. "Some fellow — drunk — was shooting up Solary's barroom," he muttered. "Dad tried to stop him."

Devlin nodded. "An' the drunk shot him an' got away. A stranger, of course, on a fast horse. Just came an' went, an' nobody ever saw him before. Yeah, that's the way it always goes." To him it was a stale story. He had seen it enacted in many towns, many times, and it generally ran to the same design. Just an unwanted man lying dead, and another man who rode off cold sober and returned later to laugh about it. Just another job.

Alec stared at the gun fighter, standing tall and remote-eyed. His mouth pinched tight. "It was a plant, then? And you knew and let him go! Damn you for a cold-blooded —"

"Your dad knew it, too," Devlin cut in flatly. "He was no fool. This was his last day, an' he gambled it away. That was the way he wanted it. I never try to stop any man from doin' what he wants to do." He was stating a

134

part of the elemental code by which he lived. This was a law of the world. His world. Jungle law.

He had a jet of sympathy for young Bourne, but for Old Alec he had nothing but understanding. When a man was all washed up, it was time to gamble everything on one last throw, and step off the end of the trail without regrets. Life, as Preacher Devlin regarded it, was meant to be lived, not merely endured. He lived it, himself, and paid for it as he went along.

"You cold devil!" Alec whispered hoarsely. "I know why you let him get killed! I know what you're up to! You're a hunted man in a tight spot, and you think you see a chance here for yourself. You wanted to make sure of getting his badge, so that you can turn your blasted guns loose and then set yourself up as the man who brought law to Rainbow! The mayor and the reverend and the council — you'd get in solid with them, fool them, get them to worshiping you, put your cursed spell on them as you've already done to — somebody else! And then —"

"Young man," broke in the reverend sternly, "please —"

But Alec rushed on with his blistering accusation. "With people like these behind you, speaking for you, making a hero of you, the governor might change his mind! Might believe you've turned over a new leaf, and call off his men. Then you'd be sitting pretty, wouldn't you? You'd have this town — have it in your fist, like Solary's got it now! You'd have everything you've got your eye on! Kingpin of Rainbow. Yes, and you'd pick it to the bones before you're through with it, take what

135

you wanted from it and throw away the leavings! Well, I'll put a spoke in that!"

He whirled toward the mayor and councilmen. "I want my dad's job — right now!"

"Y'know," Devlin remarked, unruffled, "you get pretty good ideas for a young fellow. Not bad at all. I'll think that over!"

Mayor Peattie evaded the hot young eyes. "Now, Alec!" he protested. "You're young, an' you got no experience. Anyway, your own dad gave Devlin his badge, an' you saw him do it. He knew it's a job for a gun-fighting town tamer, not an . . . uh . . . amateur, so to speak."

The reverend, still stern from his experience with violent death, laid a hand on Devlin's sleeve. "I am going to try to do what he wanted done," he stated quietly. "We must have law before we can hope for anything else."

The little man meant every word of it. He'd walk out there and get himself beaten up or killed for his principles. There was a high, steadfast courage in him, founded upon an ideal. Devlin pinned the badge to his lapel.

"Reverend," he murmured, "for a peaceful little pilgrim, you can deal me more trouble than the Texas Rangers! Bourne, hang another gun on yourself. Seeing you're so hot to bite somebody, I'm making you my deputy! What's that paper you're waving, mayor?"

"A copy of the town bylaws."

"Yeah? What's the first on it?"

" 'Thou shalt not kill'!" said the reverend.

136

"Hm-m-m? Here, let me see that list!"

"You will not find it there," rejoined the reverend. "I mean, if we must have violence, let it be only in self-defense. That badge is not a license to kill. Do you agree?"

Devlin didn't exactly, but he shaped his course to his company. "We'll let the Concordia crowd take a vote on that," he hedged. "You stay here, reverend. C'mon, Bourne, let's get to work!"

He was first out into the street, and he struck directly for the Concordia, his long legs striding fast, his ranging gaze whipping at all points. "Shoot when you have to, but don't scatter your lead," he muttered briefly to Alec. "Take your time, make sure of your man, an' don't get rattled if he's blazing at you. You'll last longer!"

It was a primary hint in gun technique from master to pupil, and young Bourne, recognizing it as such, accepted it with a nod despite his unrelenting hostility.

"I'm siding you in this, Devlin," Alec said thinly. "I'll go all the way with you. But when we're through, if we're still alive, we're going to have a showdown! You'll have to kill me, to take this town — or to take that girl — and when you do that, it'll sure show you up for what you are!"

"Pull your guns, an' shut up!" grunted Devlin. "Here goes!"

He kicked the batwing doors wide open before him, and they stamped into the Concordia. The swift suddenness of it all was no accidental impulse on

Devlin's part. A fighting man, he had a thorough appreciation for the element of surprise.

Chairs scraped noisily and a pile of poker chips spilled to the floor. Men at the long mahogany bar banged down their glasses and spun around. Stampede Solary, at a table with the Brindle Kid and Blackfoot Roen, shot to his feet with the rest. His keen face twitched, and for an instant his eyes flickered like blue flames. But this was a man with his temper and emotions enslaved by a strong intellect. He sat down again, slowly, and with the return of control he was again impassive and faintly mocking.

Devlin's hands were on his crossed belts, spreading open his long black coat. He was a Colt king, and reminding them of it. Purposely arrogant, domineering, his harsh voice cracked at them. "Line up, you two-bit bad men — the law's here!"

His right hand slipped through a rapid motion, and a gun appeared in it and thudded once. A house dealer, sitting alone with a solitaire game spread at this slack hour, bowed his head and drew his hands from beneath the table.

"Watch out for that bartender, Bourne," Devlin warned. "He's ducked under the bar, an' I don't figure he's getting us a drink!"

Alec paced toward the bar. "Show yourself, Hugo! Show yourself or —" He fired, and Hugo, peering around the far end of the bar, over a shotgun, lost his weapon and got his face full of splinters.

"Nice shot," Devlin commented, and decided that young Bourne had possibilities in him. "We'll jail that one! You haven't got those bylaws with you, huh? Never mind, we'll make up our laws as we go along! First — no gambling allowed. It's demoralizing to honest ambition!"

He threw a shot at a faro layout. The faro box, struck squarely, whirred through the air, shedding cards in its flight. He put a hole through a green baize dice table, blew the dice cup apart, and shot up a roulette wheel. And still Solary sat doing nothing, dead-panned, making no sign to his hirelings and saloon satellites. Devlin was disappointed. What he'd come for was a blazing fight and an excuse to settle matters with Solary, the Kid, and Roen. What he wanted was a town roughly cleaned up in a hurry. He had drawn and used only one gun, and now he paused to reload it, tempting them to take a chance while he was thus occupied.

But they were not to be tempted. They knew all about the other gun under his coat, and with what blinding speed it could leap out. And Alec's shot at the bartender had been fast enough to impress them. For perhaps the first time, Alec Bourne was being eyed as a dangerous man, and he had two guns out.

Devlin snapped the cylinder shut on his gun with a flirt of his wrist. He let the hammer down on a shell, and the big back-bar mirror suffered. The next bullet took care of the front window. The barroom crowd breathed hard, and the Brindle Kid began to show his teeth, but Stampede Solary deftly rolled himself a cigarette and lighted it as if nothing were happening.

"I'm out to break you, Solary!" Devlin informed the Concordia owner.

"I'm a patient man, Devlin," was all Solary said, and went on smoking.

"Bourne, is this place licensed?" Devlin queried. "No? All right, Solary, that'll cost you another church donation. A thousand dollars. Pay up!"

He was annoyed when Solary carefully counted out the money and laid it down. Bourne collected it and tucked it away. Devlin played another card. "Now I'm takin' your license away for lettin' a man get shot in here! Bar's closed. Open it, serve one drink, an' I'll burn the damned joint down! *Sabe?* Bourne, what else does this tinhorn own?"

"The Double S Hotel, the Star Dance Hall, the —"

"*Bueno!* Let's see what good we can do to *them*!"

They backed out, and at Devlin's last sight of him, Solary was blowing smoke rings and smiling faintly.

CHAPTER
SIX

Returning from putting the blight upon everything in town under the ownership of Solary — and obtaining therefrom no satisfactory fatalities — Devlin thought of Solary's placer workings on Contention Creek.

"What's this about Solary robbing you of those placer workings?" he asked Alec. They were stalking alertly along the main street, scanned wide-eyed from behind windows. Rainbow had not undergone such a devastating plague of law in all its history, not even in its pre-Concordia era, and it was somewhat dazed.

Alec sent Devlin a censorious stare. "I knew you'd get gold on your mind before long! What I said still stands!"

"It's beginning to," Devlin affirmed thoughtfully. "Maybe you're right, at that. Maybe my chance is right here in this town. Well, I'm a gambler. I play the cards as they come. Take my advice an' don't get in my way!"

"I meant what I said, Devlin! You're doing a big job, and that's all right. But when you try to take over this town for yourself, you'll have to kill me first!"

Devlin shifted his cigar and spat. "Too bad. Now tell me about those workings."

"Part of the creek belonged to my dad, from when he was in cattle," Alec recounted. "I found placer gold on it, and for a while I worked it on a small scale, with a homemade sluice box. But there's heavy black sand mixed in that creek dirt, and it clogs the riffle board. I couldn't separate the gold dust from it at first, but I finally hit on a way. Gold is heavier than lead, but the black sand isn't, so I used molten lead as a separator. Just fed the concentrate — the black sand and gold — into a pot of hot lead. Sure enough, the gold dust sank to the bottom, leaving the black sand floating on top where I could scrape it off. All I had to do then was cool the hot lead, saw off the bottom, and I had a chunk of practically pure gold, see?"

"You do get ideas," observed Devlin. "How did Solary bust you?"

Alec shrugged. "He was new here, and I didn't know he was crooked. He offered to put up the cash for a big gold washer and recovery outfit like my little one. I got my dad to give him the title to that land, to hold as security on the loan. Soon's I'd got the outfit built, somebody blew it up one night. Solary, of course. I couldn't pay back his loan, then, so he took the property, built another outfit just like mine, brought in gunmen to work and guard it, and now he owns the town. More gold was found farther along the creek, and it started a rush, but Solary rules the roost. The little wildcat miners have to sell their black-sand concentrate to him at his price, and he recovers the gold from it with my idea, at a whale of a profit. Any time a wildcat miner strikes a rich deposit, Solary's thugs rig a fight on him and take his workings. Everybody knows what's going on, but nobody's been able to do anything about it."

They were coming abreast of the Concordia. Solary stood on the low porch, and with exaggerated politeness he inclined his head to them. "Had a busy morning . . . ah . . . gentlemen?"

"Fair," said Devlin. "You're closed up all over town. Open any place o' yours, an' we burn it!"

Solary gestured unconcernedly. "I think I can afford to lose business for a day or two." He smiled, but his eyes were like marble. He let his voice sink to a monotone. "And I can well afford to outwait you, Devlin! You've got to go soon. You can't last! I'll give you no excuse to gun me. When the trigger fools are dead, and you're gone, I'll still be here to ramrod this town! You're a fighting tiger, Devlin, but patience is one thing you can't fight and beat!" He bowed again, and turned back into his empty saloon.

"Darned if I don't believe he's on the right track!" Alec allowed grudgingly.

Devlin nodded. "Yeah. But maybe we can rig a collision on him yet!"

They entered the Bourne house, and it was silent. The mayor and councilmen had departed, and the Topcliffs had apparently gone with them.

"I guess they expected trouble to bust out, and took to cover," speculated Alec.

But Devlin's mind was tackling a problem and getting a hold on it. Right now he wasn't interested in the comings and goings of municipal or spiritual fathers, or their daughters, either.

"Listen," he said. "Those wildcat miners oughtn't to have any special liking for Solary, from what you say. Now, you take a pasear down the creek an' here an' yon. Spread the word that I'm organizing a vigilante company to protect their interests an' fight Solary to a standstill!"

Alec's head came up. "By thunder, I could pretty near admire you, Devlin!" he vowed. "So now it's vigilantes, is it? 'To protect their interests,' huh? To help *your* interests, more like it! It'll make you the head of a regular law army, won't it? You're sure building your fences against the coming of the storm!"

Devlin eyed him absently, hardly listening, mentally shaping up what he hoped would be a whirlwind campaign that would either free him of this town or make the town his. "What're you waiting for?" he demanded. "Get busy — pronto!"

They began coming in small groups, the volunteer vigilantes, some nervous, some belligerent, but all hopeful that Stampede Solary's day was going into eclipse. The high-handed shutting down of Solary's various town businesses had made a tremendous impression. The talk already had it that the law was spurred by a mild little clergyman who had reformed the most notorious long rider in the territory and placed him on the side of the law. The wildcat miners were perfectly amenable to climbing aboard the

144

winning side, provided that they could see sufficient evidence that it would, without fail, be winner.

And Preacher Devlin looked like a winner, big and tough, his knee-length coat and wide-brimmed black hat giving him a strangely arresting air of somber austerity, and with a reputation higher than Hangman's Peak. So they crowded into the house and looked expectantly to him to produce a few miracles, preferably with Solary's scalp attached thereto. He looked them over, and he thought them pretty run-of-the-mill material. But these were the cards upon which he had to stake everything, win or lose, and he had to play his hand out to a finish. It had to be done today, and quickly at that. It would be only a matter of hours now before the governor's hunters closed in.

There had been no possibility of keeping this vigilante movement a secret from the Concordia crowd. News of it was all over town. They were saying that the Preacher and the little reverend were going to lead them into a kind of war of salvation, that they would clean out the town, and give it law and a church. Meantime, Solary and the Concordia crowd showed no signs of making a move, and Devlin liked that least of all.

Mayor Peattie and his three councilmen arrived last, with a few more placer miners and old citizens trailing after them. Alec, beginning to look worried, inquired about the Topcliffs.

The mayor shook his head. "They ain't been with us. They were here when we left, soon after you went out to tend to Solary. The reverend ought to be here, time like this. Maybe they're fixing their wagon. He said something about taking the wagon box off, so he could haul lumber for the —"

"Say, Devlin!" called a man at the door. "Everybody says you've clamped down tight on Solary, but it sure don't look that way! Why, his Star Dance Hall is wide open! An' listen to that piano goin' full blast! Huh!"

There was a general move toward the door, and a lot of muttered comment. The Star was open, sure enough, and nothing private about it. Devlin narrowed his eyes a little. Something was in the wind, and Solary was raising it. This was direct and open defiance, a challenge. It had to be handled at once, or the amateur vigilantes would waver, lose confidence, and drop away. A strong hand had to be shown here. Devlin jerked his head at Alec.

"C'ome on, deputy!"

They entered the Star, the vigilantes strung out behind them. There wasn't much of a crowd inside; just the Solary men, and spangled girls who belonged here. But the bar was open, and a fellow was banging the piano, and there was some dancing.

Solary was on the floor. He was dancing with a girl whose head came only as high as his shoulder. It was a waltz that they were doing, sedately enough. Solary must have heard the tramping boots of the incoming party, but he danced the girl gracefully around, and when she completed a half circle, those entering could see her face.

It was Faith Topcliff.

Devlin heard Alec make a sound as if gagging on hot chili, and a few startled grunts came from the miners. Solary, feigning to notice the newcomers for the first time, left the girl and came sauntering over. "Greetings, gentlemen!"

"What's she doing in here?" Alec blazed at him.

"Who? Oh — the Topcliff girl." Solary polished his fingernails. "She wants to work for me, so I'm trying out her dancing."

"You damned liar! Where's the reverend?"

Solary laughed softly. "Haven't you heard? Ah, well, the law is always last to hear of the crime!" He glanced over the huddle of miners. "The so-called *Rev.* Topcliff has skipped town with the . . . ah . . . church funds! Yes, Devlin, your pious little accomplice in crime sneaked out on you and took the loot with him!"

"You liar!" Alec called him again, white-faced. "It's crazy! He wouldn't desert his daughter, in any case!"

"Don't worry; she knows her way around," Solary murmured, and twisted his lips cynically. "How do you know she's his daughter?" he sneered, and dodged as Alec swung at him.

Solary was fast. He eluded the blow, and darted a hand to his hip, but brought it away empty after a lightning look at Devlin. "You poor fools!" he spat at the miners. "So you'd let yourselves be taken in by a pious little crook, and a gun-slinging outlaw on the make, and an innocent-faced little —"

Devlin swung this time, and he didn't miss. He nearly stood Solary on his head, and then he flipped out a gun. When nobody took him up on that, he reached up and yanked down one of the ornate brass ceiling lamps. He crashed the lamp to the floor, broke its oil reservoir with his heel, and took out a match.

"I'm burnin' down this joint, as I promised!" he growled, and set light to the spilled oil. "Outside, everybody, or cook!" With one blaze started, he went through the dance hall setting others, while the crowd fought their way out in a hurry.

When Devlin emerged, he found himself between a flaming dance hall and an angry mob. The wildcat miners were in an ugly state of mind. Disillusioned, regarding themselves as having been duped, they were venting their bitter abuse on the nearest scapegoat handy, who happened to be Faith.

The girl was in the midst of them, and they were accusing her of being things she'd never even heard of, and fixing worse names onto the absent reverend. Solary, still groggy from Devlin's clout, was being supported by some of his men. He was motioning toward the girl, and mumbling through broken teeth, trying to get it across to his men that he wanted the girl taken in off the street. Blackfoot Roen and a bouncer named Otto got the idea and started for her, but Alec reared up from somewhere under the crowd's feet and he was ahead of them.

Devlin took a forward step, but paused as he saw Alec fighting his way to Faith. It was better, that way. Let young Bourne loom big in the girl's eyes, for a change. He watched Alec slam down a hefty miner who disputed his way, decided that the young man was qualified to take care of himself, and transferred his attention to Roen and Otto. Those two were plowing toward the girl from a different direction. A miner, shaking a finger in the frightened face of the girl and hollering at the top of his voice, quit suddenly as Alec got there and landed on him. Alec caught hold of the girl, and she clung to him as to a lone savior in a world gone berserk. A roar went up and the crowd pressed tighter. Mob violence was breaking loose, mad and unreasoning.

Smoke from the burning building rolled over their heads, but did nothing to cool them off. Alec was battling all comers now, trying to hold a space for the girl. Blackfoot Roen and Otto, having got as far as they could through the jammed pack, drew their guns and lashed out with the barrels. They shoved on, and Otto, rising up on his toes, bobbed his round head sidewise for a better view of Alec, and attempted to take aim at him.

Alec had got about as far as he was going to get with his rescue, single-handed. Devlin didn't figure to leave him there, but he didn't incline toward joining him, either. He pitched one shot at Otto, and two into the mass of legs nearest him. The bouncer took no further interest in lining his sights on Alec, but the crowd held him wedged, and for a while he was like a man sleeping on his feet. Somebody yelped with a bullet burn on his foot, and another man fell out of the pack, hopping on one leg. Three more rapping reports and the mob split apart, permeated by a sudden instinct for self-preservation. Alec came charging out of the ruckus with Faith practically carried under one arm.

"Head for home with her, boy, where she belongs!"
Devlin sang out, and came down off the dance-hall
porch. He hit and broke through the crowd like a
thunderbolt and caught up with Alec and Faith. The
three of them were piling into the Bourne house by the
time shots began cracking from the Solary squad.

"Well, there goes our law army! Fort up, Bourne;
lock the rear!" Devlin slammed the front door and
bolted it. "Here they come — Solary's boys an' those
damned vigilante mutineers!"

Alec returned fast from locking the rear. "Wonder
where the mayor and council have gone?"

"Who, gives a hoot?" grunted Devlin. "Cussed
town's exploded, right in my face! Girl, you sure proved
good ammunition for Solary, an' he knew how to use
it." He stared dourly at Faith. "Stay out o' dance halls
after this! Where's your father?"

Faith crept closer to Alec. "He's . . . They've got him
in that thing they call a dragline bucket . . . right over a
big pot of hot lead, they said!" she gasped.

Devlin spat out the chewed remnant of his unlighted
cigar. "Hell of a place for a parson!" he muttered, and
cut loose through the front door as somebody crashed a
rock against it.

CHAPTER
SEVEN

The mob of misled miners had gone completely wild, egged on and abetted by Solary's men, who were doing most of the shooting. Windows began caving in, and Devlin got down on one knee. He spaced his shots fast, and the pair of kicking guns in his hands filled the house with their rapid roar. Reloading, he listened to the sounds outside and analyzed them. The miners, evidently losing some of their crazy belligerence in the face of that two-gun salvo, were being whipped up afresh by the Concordia bunch. Devlin could hear them being reminded of big bounty, of the reverend's alleged treachery, and of what would happen to them now if a certain long rider got the upper hand.

Alec had been talking hurriedly with Faith, and he crawled over the floor to Devlin. "We've got to get out of here!" he exclaimed. "We've got to get to the creek!"

Devlin snapped shut his loaded guns. "That's a constructive idea! How'd the reverend get himself into that dragline bucket?"

"They tricked him," Alec explained. "Faith says she and her father were trying to take the wagon box off their wagon, so they could use the wagon bed and team to haul lumber for the church. The Brindle Kid and some others came over and helped. Said they were sorry for what happened last night and wanted to make amends. And the reverend believed them!"

"He would!"

"Then they offered to show him where there was a lot of cut lumber he could have, and he went off with them to look at it. He had the team hitched up and wanted to drive there, but they said the timber was down in the creek and would have to be snaked out first. Later, Otto came and told Faith that her father was in some trouble and Solary wanted to see her about it. She ran over to Solary, and he told her that the Brindle Kid was threatening to burn her father alive!"

"Didn't even incriminate himself, huh?" Devlin scowled.

"That hombre's just too careful to live!"

"The Brindle Kid's got the reverend tied up in that big dragline bucket, Solary told Faith;" Alec rushed on. "They've got it right over the hot-lead recovery outfit, and that big bucket's got a trap-door bottom; just a jerk of a rope throws it open. They can drop him in any time!"

"An' that'd be the end o' the reverend — bone, hide an' hair!" Devlin appended grimly. "Wouldn't be a smudge left of him in that melted lead. He'd just vanish. So Solary held that over the girl, an' made her dance to his tune, huh?"

"Sure. He said he could stop the Brindle Kid, if she'd do as he told her. He made her go into the Star, waited till the miners gathered here, then pulled that stunt on us. Faith didn't dare speak up, on account of her father. Devlin, we've got to get to the creek! We've got to!"

Devlin could appreciate the necessity of that, without it being yelled in his ear. He realized, too, the length to which Solary would be prepared to go to keep the truth of the reverend's disappearance from getting out. Letting Faith get out of his hands after the dance-hall frame-up had been the only slip Solary had made so far, and that had been due to his grogginess from a healthy slam in the teeth. Right now, the only bright spot in the picture for Devlin was his remembrance of getting in that clout. He fired through a broken window at the alley across the way, and drew in exchange a spattering hail that sent him closer to the floor.

"Well, we can't take root here, that's certain," he allowed. "Get to the back, you two, an' duck out that way if the chance comes."

"How would a chance come?" Alec wanted to know. "This house is covered from all —" He paused at the glimmer in Devlin's eyes. "Man! You're not stepping out there to —"

"This is no time for explanations!" Devlin barked at him. "Do as I tell you — get!"

They left for the rear, and Devlin moved over to the couch, where the body of Old Alec still lay covered with a blanket. He had a notion that what he was about to do might meet with objections from Alec, if the young man saw it. Some folks were inclined to be squeamish about their dead. Sentiment was all right in its proper

153

place, but Devlin didn't consider that it should be allowed to stand in the way of more realistic values.

Still, as he dressed the body in his own hat and coat, he voiced a concession to conventional taste. "No disrespect to you, old-timer," he muttered. "You just happen to be needed for one more job. All things considered, you shouldn't mind givin' a hand here."

He carried the body to the front door, and pulled back the bolt.

The opening of the door threw the noise of the street into a tense moment of waiting hush. Except for the scrape and rustle of men scrambling to closer cover, the sounds of the town dwindled to less than normal, lacking even the steady rumble of Solary's power-driven concentrator from down along the creek.

Then the figure appeared inside the opened door — long-coated body in a crouch, black-hatted head bent forward. Close to its sides a pair of guns opened up with a thudding burst, and the narrow margin of silence was shattered. From every vantage point along the street, shots poured at the lone, menacing figure. The pounding impact of the bullets could be heard striking it, and it lurched over and fell asprawl across the doorstep.

"Got him! The Preacher's down!"

The exultant cry rose to a clamor up and down the street, reaching to all parts of the town. It was echoed by fighters and neutrals alike, and relayed by those out of sight of the deed.

"The Preacher's down!"

154

Men swarmed from cover, eyeing the stilled figure, and laughing with a tinny, nervous ring from their sudden letdown of tension. Others came running from all quarters to see for themselves, and the street became the convergent tryst for the town, its focal point the fallen man.

Alec was easing out via the back door, with Faith, when Devlin came up behind him.

"Devlin!" Alec gulped. "But . . . but they're all yelling that you're killed! Listen to 'em!"

"I never listen to rumors. C'me on, let's head for that wagon!" With the long reach of his legs, Devlin led the way. Stripped of his ministerial coat and hat, he looked somewhat younger despite the flecks of gray over his temples; and yet he seemed even taller, more lithe and powerful — a man panther with smooth muscles rippling under a white shirt that darkened his hard and sardonic face by contrast. The sunlight winked on the polished butts of his guns in their strapped-down holsters, and on the double loops of brass shells studding the broad black leather of his crossed belts.

And even now Alec Bourne flinched a little to see Faith's candid and impressionable young eyes fixed on that masterful, virile animal of a man. It was a case of helpless fascination. The girl could see nobody else whenever that gun-fighter warrior was around.

They tore through the back yard, passed the fence, and a slow-footed miner lumbering for the street shied off from them with a shrill yell. Devlin leaped and struck him down, but the harm was done. The yell had caught the attention of other tardy ones who hadn't yet

155

reached the street, and these looked back to discover the cause.

A shout went up. "Hey, everybody! They're gettin' out through the —"

Another shout, this time from the street, cut across the alarm. "Hell, this ain't Devlin layin' here!"

The mules were as the reverend had left them when he went off with the Brindle Kid, harnessed and hitched to the skeleton frame of the wagon bed, ready to haul lumber. They were cocking their ears at the noise, and they rolled wicked eyes snakily at Devlin as he raced toward them. Having been spoiled by the reverend's coaxing methods, they planted their legs stubbornly as Devlin sprang over a front wheel and scooped up the lines. But the Preacher wasn't in any kind of coaxing humor. He barely gave Alec and Faith time to scramble aboard before bringing the whip down with a whistling crack, and he spoke words familiar to the ears of any hardened mule.

The mules took off like scared cats, and the wagon bed bounced and swayed over the rough ground, its three riders clinging to it. Men came spilling from between buildings lining the street. Devlin chopped a shot at a Solary group, and flattened out on the jolting frame to attend to his driving. A stake and rider fence loomed up dead ahead, inclosing somebody's vegetable garden, but the Preacher was in too much of a hurry to go around it. He put a gap in the fence and a scarred track across the garden, smashed the team through the next fence, and got it headed in the direction of the creek.

The creek was empty of miners, and no faces stared up at the wagon careening along the rim trail, but a knot of men lounging at the foot of the promontory on the far side jumped up to scan it. Devlin recognized one of them as the Brindle Kid, and the others as some of the guards he had seen before around Solary's gold-recovery outfit. At their backs, atop the promontory, stood the recovery outfit, the flue of the firebox pouring smoke, and the dragline bucket suspended ready for its contents to be dumped into the short chute leading into the mammoth lead pot.

There had been no way of coming up on that side of the creek with the wagon, for no trail ran there and the ground was cut by arroyos. To take it on foot would not have been possible. Even with the running mules and lightened wagon, they had made it up the rim trail only a jump ahead of pursuit. Every man able to get hold of a horse was coming tearing out from town in the dusty wake of the wagon. Alec was looking back and throwing long shots, trying to discourage pursuit.

But Devlin was sending looks at another band of horsemen, coming up from the south and changing their course to head off the wagon. They rode in the manner of men with a purpose, and he thought of lawmen and bounty hunters. He braced himself and hauled on the lines when nearly above the power-driven concentrator on the bench, opposite the rocky promontory. Wrenching and sawing, he forced the mules to a standstill. By that time the band of horsemen was riding up close. They had the stamp of cattlemen, but were all heavily armed, and Devlin saw Mayor Peattie and the councilmen among them.

"Where you going, Devlin?" Peattie shouted. He waved an arm at the riders with him. "It looked like a riot when we left, but we ran into these fellows coming in to see —"

"We aim to join this here vigilante comp'ny we've heard about," broke in a cowman impatiently. "Where is it?"

"Coming up the pike, looking for my scalp!" Devlin grunted. Plucking a rifle from the nearest rider, he took quick aim over the creek. The Brindle Kid and the others with him were running up the promontory. They could see the crowd pouring up the rim trail from town, and the cowmen, and they evidently figured that it was high time to dispose of the reverend. One of them, well ahead of the rest, reached for the piece of rope dangling from the trapdrop floor of the dragline bucket.

Devlin's rifle cracked, fetchnig up rattling echoes from down in the deep cleft of the creek. The reaching man missed his grab, and stumbled on around the brick firebox without trying again. Devlin levered a fresh shell into the breech.

"Take these hombres an' try holding that mob back for a spell!" he called to Peattie. "Watch out for Solary's boys among 'em!"

Alec was sliding down the steep bank to the wide bench below. "I'm going over on the dragline! Keep me covered, Devlin!"

158

Devlin nodded after him. "Don't let go," he warned. "It's a long drop down!"

The mayor gaped bewilderedly. "What's Alec gonna do that for?" he blurted.

"The Kid's got the reverend in that bucket, an' aims to give him a hot bath!" Devlin answered curtly, and squeezed the rifle trigger again. Another running man veered away from the dangling length of rope, and tottered a few more steps before falling. The Brindle Kid and the two left with him dropped down and began snaking their way toward their goal, taking advantage of every dip and hollow in the short course they had to traverse.

The mayor emitted a squeak of horror at the news, then he and his horse were swallowed up and borne along by the spurring cowmen. The band of riders went clattering on along the rim to stall off the town mob and appeared happy to do it. Rainbow had been a good cow town before the coming of Solary's crowd and the wildcat miners. Between the cowmen of the locality and the present citizens' majority of Rainbow there was an abiding animosity, so far held down to a simmer by the cowmen because of lack of numbers and opportunity to do anything about it.

The dragline — high above the creek bed, and running from the concentrator on the bench to the recovery outfit on the far side — began jerking and dancing under Alec's weight. He was going it hand over hand, while Faith crouched by the wagon and watched him fixedly.

Devlin, on one knee and the rifle to his shoulder, wasted no shells. The rifle was a heavy, seven-shot repeater, far more reliable than a six-gun for the job at hand. The Preacher had four shells left in the magazine and one in the breech, and three men yonder to account for. The three men had learned caution, but they were in a hurry to finish what they had to do. Devlin whipped a shot at a leg, and the owner rolled into sight, gathered impetus until helpless to stop himself, and his shriek was long and shuddery as he hurtled off the edge of the high bank down to the stony creek bed below.

The Brindle Kid and his one remaining companion got up and made a rush over the last few yards. The rifle spoke again, and then the Brindle Kid was ducking and zig-zagging alone, but he made it around the firebox and out of sight. One of his arms was in a sling, but he still had one good hand and a gun, and from behind the firebox his gun spat a tiny ball of smoke. It was tricky shooting for a short gun, but his bullet nicked the steel-strand dragline and set it humming. Alec continued his slow advance without pause, hand over hand, but the strain on his muscles could be seen to be slowing him down.

Devlin laid a bullet on the edge of the firebox and knocked a brick to chips and powder. For a moment no other move came from the Kid. Then his arm began darting upward, snatching at the piece of rope under the dragline bucket. He touched it once and set it swinging. It was just a little out of his reach, and he was trying to avoid leaving his arm exposed long enough to

160

make a target, but he was bound to get his fingers around that rope sooner or later.

Alec got above solid ground, and let go. He hit the ground, tumbled, got up, and advanced on the firebox. He dodged as the Kid's gun bobbed around the bricks and thudded at him, and threw a return shot that missed. The Kid had all the advantage of cover.

Devlin estimated angles, and lined his sights on a spot underneath the slanted iron chute that served as a feed hopper for the recovery outfit. He fired. With the clang of the iron chute, a streak of molten lead spurted from the pot, kicked up by the ricochet bullet plumping into it. There was a thin howl, and the Brindle Kid leaped up from behind the firebox, clasping and clawing at his face. With the last bullet in the rifle, Devlin dropped him back again.

Then Devlin watched Alec climb up and lift the trussed figure of the little reverend out of the dragline bucket, and he listened to the sudden roar of the mob along the rim trail as they saw that. He glanced down at the expression on Faith's face, and again at Alec with the reverend. And he thought it damnable that there was gold over yonder, that he was here on this side, and that Stampede Solary still lived.

CHAPTER
EIGHT

Stampede Solary rested both hands on the bar of his Concordia Saloon. He said softly: "You've downed my best men, kicked the works over, and got everybody shouting for you, Devlin! All right, you've got this town in your fist — but for how long?"

It was growing dark, and the lamps were lighted in the Concordia. Blackfoot Roen sat at a table by himself, doing nothing, saying nothing. Men sat around other tables, as idle and unmoving as Blackfoot. No drinks were being served, and no games played.

Preacher Devlin, his usual saturnine self once more in his long, black coat and hat, retrieved from Alec Bourne's body, helped himself from a cigar box and threw down a dollar. "I may be around for quite a while," he mentioned. "The reverend, the mayor an' council, the cowmen and even all the miners — they're all ready to side me against the governor. They're ready to swear I cleaned up this town an' it can't get along without me. Maybe you better pull stakes, Solary!"

Solary smiled, shaking his head. "You can't pin a thing on me. My bar's closed and so are the games. I'm in line with the law to the last inch. I'll go on playing it that way, and I'll make no errors. Can you say the same thing for yourself? You're the kingpin of Rainbow right now, yes — but only just so long as you tread a tight law line! Step off that line, and you're out! You know that. You've clamped more law onto this town than you can live by, yourself! Some day you'll break loose. All this is only a flash in the pan. I'm a patient man, as I've said before. I won't have so long to wait. You'll be just a memory — but I'll be the real thing again!"

With a cigar between his teeth, Devlin strolled out, and Solary called mockingly after him: "Maybe you better pull stakes, Preacher!"

To himself, Devlin admitted that Solary held a pretty good ace card, there. Played that way, it would take a long time to dislodge Solary and make the town permanently safe for the reverend and other peaceful folks like him. Solary knew how to wait and keep his hands clean, pending the time when he could reach out and take hold of Rainbow again. And the longer that time was delayed, the more coldly virulent would be his vengeance on those who had worked against him. His patience was of that kind, keeping sharp the cutting edge of his cruelty and his lust for power.

On the street, Devlin found himself joined by the reverend, Faith and Alec. As if reading the gun fighter's mood, the reverend spoke of Solary. "He is a menace to the peace of this town," he conceded. "But he is afraid of you, and he'll commit no harm as long as you are here. You'll stay, won't you? Whatever has happened in your past is done and gone, and we are all very willing to make it possible for you to remain here."

That same idealistic glow was in his eyes, promising determined help in reformation. And that different look, that soft shine, came creeping back into Faith's eyes. It seemed to come back without her consent, for she was very young, so young that fascination could bewilder her into believing it was something deeper — so young that she did not know how to control its coming or its unpredictable consequences.

"Please stay!" she said, and the words were involuntary, containing more in their tone than in their bare meaning.

And then at last the reverend looked at his daughter, a little startled at first, then sharply, and finally with dismay. In an unnatural voice he said to Alec: "Will you please see Faith home?"

Alec nodded stiffly. "Sure." He, too, had witnessed the fleeting recurrence of that look.

They walked off, and the reverend said, looking after them: "I like to see those two together. I believe they love each other, and will discover it soon — if nothing blinds them off the natural path. All they need is a chance. That would be best wouldn't it?"

Devlin nodded. "Yeah, that'd be all right. G'night, reverend." He strode off, leaving the churchman gazing troubled after him.

An hour later the swing doors of the Concordia parted wide open, nearly torn off their hinges by a hefty kick. They flapped back again, slapped the kicker before he cleared them, and for a brief spell he got tangled up with them. A growled oath, a protesting shriek of mangled hinges, and one of the doors went sailing into the street while its mate came banging and sliding over the barroom floor.

Solary jerked up straight, Blackfoot Roen scraped back his chair, and the half dozen others in the barroom clumped to their feet. Their eyes widened and then narrowed, fastened on the tall, disheveled intruder standing spread-legged in the doorway. They needed nobody to tell them what this was. Here was a bad man on a whale of a bender, a curly wolf all lit up and hitting the high spots, celebrating a Colt coronation and kingship over everything within range of his shooters. It was an impressive sight.

Devlin's wide-brimmed ministerial hat was tipped at a rakish slant. His shirt collar was open, and the long coat was thrust back, hands shoved into the broad cartridge belts. He stood swaying gently, one black eyebrow up, the other down, taking survey of the saloon's interior.

"More life in a graveyard!" was his comment, and his voice was thick and slurred.

He removed one hand from his belts and stuck a thumb over his shoulder. "What the hell d'you want doors for, anyway? This joint's never closin' from here on, nor any other bottlery in my territory! This is my town, an' that's an order! Y'hear me? *My* town! Speak up, Solary — wherever the blazes you are!"

A bright gleam lighted Solary's eyes, but he spoke very civilly. "Right, Preacher. Anything you say goes. I'm right here behind the bar."

Devlin placed one foot forward, teetered precariously, and it seemed likely that he would depart

165

backward into the street, but the edge of the door frame saved him. After two false tries, he abandoned that support and found the bar.

"Best in the house for me!" he growled.

"Best in the house — on the house — for Preacher Devlin!" crooned Solary, and swiftly set it out.

Devlin got a hand on the bottle. "Don't you serve any glasses in this sorry, broken-down burro stable?" he demanded.

"Sure. One right by your elbow," answered Solary.

Devlin located it, picked it up, scowled at it, and tossed it contemptuously over his shoulder. "Damned eye cup! Hand me somethin' man size. A beer glass!"

He filled the glass till it ran over, emptied it in two gulps, and with the bottle and glass in his hands he inclined at a list toward the nearest table, upsetting only two spittoons and a chair in his course. He royally waved off three men who already happened to be seated there, and they vacated.

"My town! Goin' to run you out o' business, Solary! Goin' to take over this place — every place. Run 'em right. Run 'em my way —" His head drooped. He roused himself, made a swipe for the bottle, missed getting it, and knocked it to the floor. The effort pitched him forward off balance, but when his head slumped onto the table he seemed to find it comfortable there, and left it that way.

Blackfoot Roen rose silently to his feet, his leaden, humorless eyes slanted inquiringly at Solary, his hands on his gun butts. The half dozen others also rose, nodding eagerly. Solary's narrow, clever face reflected a

166

warring of thoughts and emotions. His eyes were bright with the urge of immediate opportunity. Patience was an excellent trick; it had always paid him well, and its use was in line with his careful principles for never taking any risk that could be avoided. But here was a single card that could be played to win at one stroke, right now and without risk. It was too tempting a chance to throw away. Patience lost. Solary nodded quickly and thrust a hand under his armpit.

"Let him have it!" he whispered.

A chair went flying. A table crashed over. A pair of eyes, gray as sleet and cold sober, glittered with saturnine mischief above a heavy pair of exploding, kicking guns.

By the time the town began taking stock, the Concordia was on fire. Mayor Peattie, coughing and spluttering, stumbled hastily out of the burning building after viewing the havoc inside, and his face was white.

"Four men dead in there!" he gaped to the crowd assembled outside. "Solary, Roen, Haff Torbert and Escobio. The others went through a window, from the looks of it — and still running, likely!"

"No sign of Devlin?" rapped Colonel Rorick. "Wonder where he is?"

That question was soon answered by a wild whoop and a sudden stamping of hoofs. Mounted on his own big black horse, Devlin hit the street and shot down the emporium signboard by way of announcing his arrival. In the lurid glare of the burning Concordia, even his horse wore an air of reckless frolic, entering into the graceless spirit of things with skittish cavortings, prancing around, shaking its head and showing its heels. Drunk as he appeared, Devlin rode with the easy mastery of a consummate horseman. He put the big black full at the crowd, reined it broadside with a touch, and bowled over five miners who weren't as lively in their reactions as the rest of the crowd.

"Get out o' here, you worthless creek scabblers! This is my town an' I'll have my fun with it! Mine, *sabe?* Tomorrow I'll be coming around to collect special taxes, first thing. Be ready to pay out! Now vamoose!"

He ran them off the street as if they were cattle, riding back and forth, twirling a rope and crowding them. They were manageable, and became more so when they saw the mayor and council bolting prudently for cover. With all the street his to operate in, Devlin, raising a long yell, lifted his horse onto the boardwalk and started up it at a rocking gallop.

Ducking the low-hanging signboards, hoofs hammering the loose planks, he shot out windows as he thundered by. At the far end of the street he took to the other side and came roaring back, guns blazing.

Mayor Peattie and the town council emerged with dubious authority from the store where they had taken cover. The mayor raised a hand, shaking a finger at Devlin and shouting something about law and order. Devlin shot off his hat as he careened by, and the mayor led the dash back into the store. On his next round, Devlin found one lone man waiting for him, standing planted in the street, two guns buckled on and his arms stiff at his sides.

Alec Bourne had learned something about gun technique and gun-fighter temperament. He had learned it from the man he had come out to face.

"Pull up, Devlin!" he called crisply.

Devlin reined his plunging horse to a stamping, hoof-digging halt. He cuffed back his hat and leaned on the saddlehorn. "How'ya, son!" he greeted blandly. "What brings you out?"

"If you're not too drunk, you'll remember what I said would have to be done, any time you made a grab to take over this town!" Alec's voice was even, though a little strained. "It's come sooner than I thought. You've kicked the lid off and showed yourself for what you are, and it's gone far enough!"

"Hell, I haven't started yet!"

"You're through, Devlin! This is a law-abiding town, now. There's no place in it for a gun-fighting outlaw marshal who thinks he can use it for his private playground and shoot it up when he takes the notion! The mayor and council expect me to take away your badge, or trade smoke, trying! I'm here to try!" Alec expected to die, that was certain. And the watching town expected him to die. But he would go through with it, hoping to get in a shot as he went down.

"I reckon Solary was right," Devlin said solemnly. "I brought more law to this town than I could live up to, myself. So they want me to quit, huh? Is that what the reverend says, too?"

"Yes!"

Devlin nodded. He plucked the badge from the lapel of his coat, and tossed it to Alec. It was the first time that he had ever backed down before any man's challenge, but he did it without regret. He drew an envelope from his coat pocket. "Here's something else you can have — your deed to that creek land. I took it from Solary's safe when I set fire to the Concordia. Got the key from his pocket. Seemed a waste to let that paper burn with the trash. S'long, son — an' good luck!"

He heeled the black and went clattering down the street and out of town, leaving Alec staring after him and the town in a buzz of astonishment.

Along the rim trail Devlin found the Rev. Topcliff, mounted on one of his mules, and he pulled up alongside.

"Sorry, reverend," he said gruffly. "I reckon you won't be seeing me in your Sunday congregation."

Darkness made the reverend's face unfathomable. "Wherever you may go, I shall always see you in my congregation," he said quietly. "I wanted you to know that, before you left." He held out his right hand. "Good-by, good friend — and my blessings go with you for everything that you've done here."

He might have kept that town in his fist, if he'd wanted it, and been its permanent kingpin, Devlin know. Ah, well — He shrugged, and misquoted a line that came into his mind. "'Better a beggar on horseback, than catch the conscience of a tyrant king!'"

Not quite a beggar, though. Not exactly. He patted a well-filled pocket. There had been other things in Stampede Solary's safe, besides the deed, which it would have been a waste to let burn with the trash.

170